倍斯特出版事業有限公司
Best Publishing Ltd.

IELTS 雅思聽力聖經

Amanda Chou ◎ 著

英式發音
MP3

真題重現 近 **1400** 題 超值演練
直取聽力 **8** 分

學習彈性和銜接性強，補足傳統模擬試題學習侷限

將官方試題分拆成三個階段：「**核心能力和影子跟讀覆誦**」、「**填空測驗和拼字強化**」
以及「**全真試題**」，各程度考生均適用且馬上建立信心。

根據大腦思考路徑 多一道規劃，有效突破7.5魔咒關卡

包含「**聽力整合能力＋全真試題**」，有效改善練習無數官方試題仍未反應在應試分數上
的窘境，提升**核心基礎能力**、**思考力**和**反應力**，即刻獲取8分佳績。

作者序

　　在許多考試的備考，考生都知道要寫近十年的考古題以熟悉跟掌握這項考試的規律性，但是在經過名師講解歷屆試題後，對大多數的考生來說，成效仍是裹足不前，因為當中牽涉到許多因素。以物理科來說，歷屆試題每題都包含了多種單元的概念在裡面，可能包含 2-4 種物理概念考驗考生的綜合能力，也因為如此就更難憑藉只演練考古題並且在經由名師講解後，考生就能在學校的模擬試題考試或指考測驗中一次性從低標的分數考到均標或是從均標的分數考到前標。這些試題的設計可能同包含了摩擦力、力學和浮力等章節的概念在。

　　這項推理也能在雅思測驗中找到痕跡。在更之前的考試更是如此，因為在更之前劍橋雅思官方系列只出到 7-9，每次的真題都極為珍貴是拿來考前演練用的，而不是平常演練，因為會浪費掉試題。儘管現在出到了 15，以聽力來說 40 分鐘能寫完一回聽力測驗（一本官方試題總共會包含 4 回完整的聽力測驗），所以即使有 15 本劍橋雅思試題也會很快的就寫完，但寫完且經由名師講解後，仍不能保證你能在實際考試中考到理想成績，更可能在準備 3-6 個月後仍考取同樣的成績。就像是你

這次新多益測驗考了 870 分好了，你預期在寫 10 回坊間出版社出版的模擬試題後，只要聽力或閱讀多對幾題就能達到 900 分，但卻在準備過後考取同樣的分數或是考到了 875 分，而事與願違。這是因為試題是有效度在的，當然也牽涉到很多影響因素，例如你的核心能力等並未因寫完 10 回試題後就有所提升，寫試題只是一直增加對該考試的熟悉度。

回到物理測驗，如果有另一個學習模式或是家教針對或設計了重理解力，且將 2-4 種合起來的概念都分拆開的一系列題目，考生確實理解了當中單獨的浮力等的概念，並持續演練 2 種概念結合的題目，甚至到 3-4 種，考生就不會淪為試題仍解到某個步驟，但卻因為第 3 種概念或第 4 種概念的加入，而還是無法算對某個數字，在無論是物理選擇題或是非選擇題都還是無法得分，而在準備後仍事與願違地考取相同的成績。

在雅思測驗中亦是如此，對大多數考生來說，在聽力核心能力沒提升前，直接寫官方試題所發揮的效用很有限，只是熟悉試題，聽不懂的

部分仍是沒有聽懂，可能寫下了許多詳盡的備考計畫，例如一份 excel 表確實記錄了寫劍橋雅思 1-15，共 60 回聽力測驗所答對的題數，可能得到的都是某個範位的數字，或少數稍高的數字，但不是欲達到理想成績的答對題數，這也間接傳遞了一項訊息，以這樣的計畫要在應考獲取理想成績是有些牽強的。考生應將重點放在提升核心能力，例如聽力專注力，在這部分的提升後再照著這個備考計畫走，就能快速拉高成績了。

在書籍中，將官方聽力測驗分拆成三個部分，而非讓考生直接寫官方試題。第一個部分是「影子跟讀法的學習」，以提升考生聽力專注力等，這部分是任何階段的學習者都能一直使用各個單元內容來反覆練習。第二個部分是「填空測驗」，用以提升考生拼字等能力。初、中階考生更能受益於這項設計，因為只要順著聽就好，也還不用直接就寫官方試題，**考生要達到這個階段所要求的能力後再進行下個階段**（也就是書籍中規劃的第三部分）。第三個部分規劃了全真試題，考生經由第一階段的核心能力強化和第二階段的聽力門檻要求後，再來演練需要經由

理解部分改寫句或定位等相關訊息的題目。也因為經過前兩階段的強化更能找到出盲點，並一舉有更具成效的聽力突破。（當然程度夠好的考生可以直接寫第三部分，但對大多數考生來說，沒有經過分拆演練，直接寫第三部分的測驗或是官方試題，無形中只是耗掉了試題或影響自己備考信心）。

　　最後要説明的是，在公司之前出版的《一次就考到雅思聽力 6.5+》和《一次就考到雅思聽力 7+》包含了大量的第一部分+第二部分的聽力規劃，有需要演練更多基礎聽力能力的考生，也能經由這兩本書累積更多聽力實力。最後祝考生都能獲取理想成績。

Amanda Chou

使用說明

INSTRUCTIONS

超給力的「雅思循環字彙」填空練習
一次性掌握生活類和學術類場景循環必考字彙

· 學術類主題精選了官方常考題，例如：**諾貝爾的生平、汽車、塗鴉、動物玩耍和飛機**等的歷史，這些都會在聽或讀的主題中循環出現，可以增加熟悉感，加速閱讀等答題速度。此外，生活類主題也納入更多生活類常考字彙，像是 telephone, refrigerator 等用字，將時間花在刀口只演練跟拼讀這些必考字彙，事半功倍攻略雅思聽力。

掌握細微、隱晦且不易答、不易定位或是同義改寫題,巧取雅思聽力八分

‧ 從填空測驗養成順著聽力內容都能聽對挖空的字後,循序漸進演練需要推敲、經由同義改寫的試題或詞性轉換題,應試時不加思索即能迅速拆解變化百端的試題,突破 7.5 魔咒。

▶ 全真模擬試題練習 🎧 MP3 001

❶ The Dutch East India Company was having a competition with two nations: _____ and _____.

❷ The Dutch also recognized the fertile _____ in the area.

❸ The so-called agricultural ventures exported wheat, _____, and _____.

❹ Two items were brought back to the west: _____ and _____.

❺ _____ were benefiting from this and earned handsome profits.

❻ A typical family meal might include three or four such dishes and _____.

❼ Fish and chips is the dish of the _____.

❽ Americans' dishes consist of _____ and fries.

Unit 1　台南－蝦米飯

❶ Spain, Portuguese

❷ soils

❸ ginger, tobacco

❹ spice, porcelain

❺ Investors

❻ soup

❼ British

❽ burger

Part 1 生活類主題

Part 2 學術類主題

▶▶ 全真模擬試題練習 🎧 MP3 037

❶ Hans Lippershey: a _____ maker

❷ 1594: settled in Middelburg in the _____

❸ _____: he immigrated in the Netherlands.

❹ 1607: filed a patent for _____

❺ interesting version: came from an _____ on children

❻ comment: make a far away weather-vane seem closer when looking at it through _____ lenses

❼ original instrument: to get an _____ image

❽ _____: he passed away

❶ spectacle

❷ Netherlands

❸ 1602

❹ telescope

❺ observation

❻ two

❼ upright

❽ 1619

掌握數字等的出題，聽對各種數字變化題
初學乍練即獲取高分成效

· 包含了各式的數字題型，從簡易的年代到 PH 酸鹼度等
　數值以及 ppm 等的數值變化題，一次性掌握各類別的
　數字考題，多對關鍵 1-2 題即考取八分。

影子跟讀學習加持
聽力專注力和理解力提升
其他高階聽力技能，定位等的能力
也隨之提高，分數就飆升

· 每個單元的第一個學習規劃，即影子跟讀學習法，以中
  英對照呈現，各階段考生均適用，且須反覆演練，對已
  經具備 7-7.5 分考生，更需要不斷練習，這部分影響到
  section 3 和 section 4 某些聽力訊息的定位，迅速解脫
  分數卡關的窘境。

種特殊的方式在告訴大家，石墨是來自中國。

It is because back in the 1800s, the best graphite in the world came from China. And the color yellow in China means royalty and respect. Only the imperial family was allowed to use the color yellow. Therefore, the American pencil companies began to paint their pencils bright yellow to show the regal feeling. Here we will be introducing Nicolas Jacques Conte who was credited as the inventor of the modern lead pencil from France.

這是因為早在 1800 年時，世界上最好的石墨來自中國。而在中國，黃色意味著皇室和尊重。只有皇室允許使用的黃色。因此，美國的鉛筆公司開始將自己的鉛筆漆成明亮的黃色，以顯示帝王的感覺。在這裡，我們將介紹尼古拉斯·雅克·康特，一位來自法國的現代鉛筆發明人。

249

UNIT 39

石墨：皇室的象徵

▶影子跟讀「短段落」練習　🎧 MP3 039

此篇為「**影子跟讀短段落練習**」，規劃了由聽「**短段落**」的 shadowing 練習，強化聽力專注力和掌握各個考點！

In 1812, a Massachusetts cabinet maker, William Monroe, made the first wooden pencil. The American pencil industry also took off during the 19th century. Starting with the Joseph Dixon Crucible Company, many pencil factories are based on the East Coast, such as New York or New Jersey. At first, pencils were all natural, unpainted and without printing company's names. Not until 1890s, many pencil companies started to paint pencils in yellow and put their brand name on it. Why yellow? Red or blue would look nice, too." You might think. It was actually a special way to tell the consumer that the graphite came from China.

1812 年，麻省的一個櫥櫃製造商，威廉·莫瑞，製作了第一個木製鉛筆。美國製筆業也是在 19 世紀起飛。由約瑟夫·狄克遜公司開始，很多鉛筆工廠都開在東岸，如紐約或新澤西州。起初，鉛筆都是天然的，沒有油漆，沒有印刷公司的名稱。直到 1890 年代，許多鉛筆公司開始把鉛筆漆成黃色，並把自己的品牌名稱印上。你可能會認為「為什麼是黃色？紅色或藍色的也很好看。」。它實際上是用一

248

▶▶ 聽、讀雙效「填空」練習 🎧 MP3 041

此部分為**聽、讀雙效「填空」練習**，現在就一起動身，開始聽「短段落」，提升常考字彙、語感等答題能力！

Back in the late 90's 1.＿＿＿＿＿ were not as common, 2.＿＿＿＿＿ could be found in every pen case and on every 3.＿＿＿＿＿. It is actually a 4.＿＿＿＿＿ of the Newell Rubbermaid company that sells 5.＿＿＿＿＿. It is not a surprise that liquid paper was invented by a 6.＿＿＿＿＿. Bette Graham who used to make many 7.＿＿＿＿＿ while working as a typist, invented the first correction 8.＿＿＿＿＿ in her 9.＿＿＿＿＿ back in 1951. Using only paints and 10.＿＿＿＿＿, G raham made her first generation correction fluid called Mistake Out and started to sell it to her 11. co-workers.

Graham for sure saw the 11.＿＿＿＿＿ with her invention and founded the Mistake Out Company back in 1956 while she was still working as a typist. However, she was later on fired from her job because of some 12.＿＿＿＿＿. Just like that, she worked from her kitchen alone for 13.＿＿＿＿＿. In 1961, the company name was changed to Liquid Paper and it was sold to the Gillette Corporation for 14.＿＿＿＿＿ in 1979.

▶▶ 參考答案

1. while computers	2. liquid paper
3. desk	4. brand name
5. correction products	6. typist
7. mistakes	8. fluid
9. kitchen	10. kitchen ware
11. business opportunity	12. silly mistakes
13. 17 years	14. $47.5 million

讓許多初、中階考生迷途知返、茅塞頓開
規劃海量填空練習
具備基礎聽力實力才寫官方試題

· 協助眾多初、中階考生演練官方試題卻未反應在分數上的問題，這些階段的考生應該要先都具備能聽對書中所有填空測驗後才練習官方試題才能發揮學習成效。

聽力和閱讀中重複出現的考點
大幅擴充考生知識面、提升應試反應力

· 降低答題的陌生感，是獲取高分的關鍵之一，藉由考古題和機
  經等的相關話題演練和音檔，同步提升聽、讀能力，發揮事半
  功倍的學習成效。

UNIT 46

動物玩耍

▶ 影子跟讀「短段落」練習 🎧 MP3 046

此篇為「影子跟讀短段落練習」，規劃了由聽「短段落」的
shadowing 練習，強化聽力專注力和掌握各個考點！

　　In today's lecture, we are going to cover more details concerning the play of young animals. The first type is locomotor play. As the word locomotor implies, this type of play strengthens muscle and physical coordination. The second type is predatory play, in which animals stalk and swoop upon playmates to mimic hunting behaviors. Even birds, such as falcons, crows, and swallows, engage in predatory play; they drop tiny objects from above and descend rapidly to catch those objects. The third type is object play, which is often played solitarily and combined with predatory play, though not always. For instance, primates, due to their adroitness, play with various objects in a similar way as human children do. Primates have been proven to demonstrate their imagination in object play. In research, a chimpanzee having been trained to use sign language placed a purse on his foot, and gave the sign for "shoe". The fourth type of play is social play, which allows animals to form friendship, learn cooperation, and mimic adult competitive behaviors without acting violently. Re-

290

Unit 46　動物玩耍

garding the benefits of play, I would like to focus on the effects on the brain. Emotionally, play just makes animals feel relaxed and less stressed. They touch one another the most when playing, and touching stimulates a chemical in the brain called opiate, which generates a soothing feeling. To sum up, there are at least four areas that play exerts positive effects on: physical, social, emotional, and intelligent areas.

　　今天的講課，我們將涵蓋更多關於年輕動物玩耍的細節。第一種類型是運動玩耍。就像運動這個字暗示的，這個類型加強肌肉和身體協調能力。第二種類型是捕食玩耍，玩耍當中動物會尾隨並突然襲擊玩伴，這是在模仿打獵行為。甚至鳥類，例如獵鷹、烏鴉和燕子，也會進行捕食玩耍。他們會從高處丟下小型物體，然後快速下降去抓那些物體。第三個類型是物體玩耍，常常是獨自進行並和捕食玩耍合併，雖然不見得總是這樣。例如，由於靈長類的肢體靈巧，他們玩各種物體的方式和人類小孩玩耍的方式是類似的。在進行物體玩耍時，靈長類已經被證實會展現想像力。在一個研究中，一隻曾受過手語訓練的黑猩猩將一個皮包放在腳上，並比出「鞋子」的手語。第四個類型是社交玩耍，讓動物建立友誼，學習合作，並模仿成年競爭性的行為，但不會展現暴力。關於玩耍的益處，我想專注在對頭腦的影響。情緒上，玩耍就是讓動物覺得放鬆，比較沒壓力。當玩耍時，他們碰觸彼此最多，而碰觸會刺激腦內一種稱為鴉片類物質的化學物質，這化學物質會產生放鬆的感覺。總之，玩耍至少在四個方面發揮正面效應：生理、社交、情緒和智能方面。

291

Part 1 生活類主題

Part 2 學術類主題

011

破解各類型英語測驗的出題
掌握關鍵字彙和語法
對各種題型均能隨機應變

‧藉由聽力填空練習，同步修正口語表達、各類型
英語考試中的詞類挖空、強化各主題的字彙能
力，內建超強語感，迅速獲取高分。

聽、讀雙效「填空」練習 🎧 MP3 046

此部分為聽、讀雙效「填空」練習，現在就一起動身，開始聽
「短段落」，提升常考字彙、語感等答題能力！

In today's lecture, we are going to cover more details concerning the play of young 1._____. The first type is locomotor play. As the word locomotor implies, this type of play strengthens 2._____ and physical 3._____. The second type is 4._____ play, in which animals stalk and swoop upon 5._____ to mimic hunting 6._____. Even birds, such as 7._____, crows, and swallows, engage in predatory play; they drop tiny 8._____ from above and 9._____ rapidly to catch those objects. The third type is object play, which is often played 10._____ and combined with predatory play, though not always. For instance, 11._____, due to their 12._____, play with various objects in a similar way as human children do. Primates have been proven to demonstrate their 13._____ in object play. In research, a 14._____ having been trained to use sign 15._____ placed a purse on his foot, and gave the sign for "shoe". The fourth type of play is social play, which allows animals to form 16._____, learn 17._____, and mimic adult 18._____ behaviors without acting 19._____. Regarding the benefits of play, I would like to focus on the 20._____ on the brain. Emotionally, play just makes animals feel relaxed and less 21._____.

292

_____. They touch one another the most when playing, and touching stimulates a 22._____ opiate, which 23._____ a soothing feeling. To sum up, there are at least four areas that play exerts positive effects on: physical, social, emotional, and 24._____ areas.

Unit 46 動物玩耍

Part 1 生活類主題

Part 2 學術類主題

參考答案

1. animals
2. muscle
3. coordination
4. predatory
5. playmates
6. behaviors
7. falcons
8. objects
9. descend
10. solitarily
11. primates
12. adroitness
13. imagination
14. chimpanzee
15. language
16. friendship
17. cooperation
18. competitive
19. violently
20. effects
21. stressed
22. chemical
23. generates
24. intelligent

293

目次 CONTENTS

Part 1　生活類主題

Part 2　學術類主題

收錄 30 篇較具深度的生活類聽力主題，
並規劃三個階段的聽力練習，反覆聽誦與
記憶，除了可以強化聽力之外，更能大幅
提升中翻英實力，在各英語課堂中均游刃
有餘。

PART 1

台南－蝦米飯
Tainan Shrimp fried rice

▶▶ 影子跟讀「短段落」練習 🎧 MP3 001

　　此篇為「**影子跟讀短段落練習**」，規劃了由聽「**短段落**」的 shadowing 練習，強化聽力專注力和掌握各個考點！

　　Some say that Tainan is the cultural and export center of the island. The city specializes in preserving Taiwanese culture, but was also once host to Fort Zeelandia – the Dutch port that was the primary city from which that country traded with E. Asia. Beginning in the early 1600s, the Dutch East India Company at what is now Tainan was trying to get a piece of the successful spice trade that Spain operated from Manila and the Portuguese operated on Macau. The Dutch also recognized the fertile soils in the area and established European style agricultural ventures, growing and exporting wheat, ginger, and tobacco. From Tainan, the Dutch not only brought much spice and porcelain back to the west, but also untold riches to the profit of their European investors. Today, Tainan is the second largest city of Taiwan. Inexpensive stir fry restaurants are found everywhere. A typical family meal – whether eaten at home or while dining out – might consist of three or four such dishes to share, plus soup. It's the classic Taiwanese alternative to the British fish and chips or the American burger and fries. Inexpensive, quickly prepared, and broadly enjoyed.

　　有人說，台南是這個島上的文化和出口中心。這個城市保有很棒的閩南文化，這裡也有安平古堡，這個港口是當時荷蘭定為主要可以與亞洲各國交易的城市。始於 17 世紀初，荷蘭東印度公司當時為了成功與占領馬尼拉的西班牙，據有澳門的葡萄牙爭奪香料貿易，而在現在的台南據點。荷蘭人知道台南地區有肥沃的土壤，建立了歐洲風格的農業企業，種植和出口小麥、生薑和煙草。荷蘭人從台南不僅把很多的香料和瓷器運回西方，同時讓他們的歐洲投資者得到很高的利潤。在台南簡單的小吃到處都有。便宜的快炒店隨處可見。一般家庭無論是在家裡吃或外出用餐，大概會有三道或四道菜一起分享，再加上一碗湯。這種典型的台灣菜就好像是英國的炸魚排和薯條或是美國的漢堡薯條。便宜、備餐迅速和廣受人喜愛。

此部分為**聽、讀雙效「填空」練習**，現在就一起動身，開始聽「短段落」，提升常考字彙、語感等答題能力！

Some say that Tainan is the 1._____ and export center of the island. The city specializes in 2._____ Taiwanese culture, but was also once host to 3._____ Zeelandia – the Dutch 4._____ that was the 5._____ city from which that 6._____ traded with E. Asia. Beginning in the early 1600s, the Dutch East India Company at what is now Tainan was trying to get a piece of the 7._____ spice trade that 8._____ operated from Manila and the 9._____ operated on Macau. The Dutch also recognized the 10._____ soils in the area and established European style 11._____ ventures, growing and exporting 12._____, ginger, and tobacco. From Tainan, the Dutch not only brought much spice and 13._____ back to the west, but also untold riches to the profit of their European 14._____. Today, Tainan is the second largest city of Taiwan. Inexpensive stir fry 15._____ are found everywhere. A 16._____ family meal – whether eaten at home or while dining out – might consist of three or four such dishes to share, plus soup. It's the classic Taiwanese 17._____ to the British 18._____ and chips or the American 19._____ and fries. Inexpensive, quickly 20._____, and broadly enjoyed.

▶▶ 參考答案

1. cultural	2. preserving
3. Fort	4. port
5. primary	6. country
7. successful	8. Spain
9. Portuguese	10. fertile
11. agricultural	12. wheat
13. porcelain	14. investors
15. restaurants	16. typical
17. alternative	18. fish
19. burger	20. prepared

❶ The Dutch East India Company was having a competition with two nations: _____ and _____ .

❷ The Dutch also recognized the fertile _____ in the area.

❸ The so-called agricultural ventures exported wheat, _____ _____ , and _____ .

❹ Two items were brought back to the west: _____ and _____ .

❺ _____ were benefiting from this and earned handsome profits.

❻ A typical family meal might include three or four such dishes and _____ .

❼ Fish and chips is the dish of the _____ .

❽ Americans' dishes consist of _____ and fries.

❶ Spain, Portuguese

❷ soils

❸ ginger, tobacco

❹ spice, porcelain

❺ Investors

❻ soup

❼ British

❽ burger

UNIT ❷

台南－鹹粥

Tainan Salty Porridge

▶ 影子跟讀「短段落」練習 🎧 MP3 002

此篇為「影子跟讀短段落練習」，規劃了由聽「短段落」的 shadowing 練習，強化聽力專注力和掌握各個考點！

Salty porridge is a classic southern Taiwan breakfast dish, enjoyed with gusto — and a fried donut stick — in Tainan. The rice and broth for this salty porridge are prepared so that the rice remains light and firm. In the common rice congee, the rice is cooked with large amounts of water long enough to make the grains so soft that they begin to break apart. Salty porridge in Tainan is made so that the clear fish broth is added over the cooked rice, seafood and any vegetables at the end of cooking. And the main ingredient of salty porridge is milkfish — a popular, mild-tasting white fish. There are many other ways that milkfish is enjoyed in Tainan — in soup, fried, and as fish balls, for example. Most Milkfish available in Taiwan is not wild-caught, but raised through aquaculture or fish farming systems. Traditionally, the fish fingerlings are caught in the open sea, then raised in ponds or under-water cages of warm, brackish coastal water. Production of milkfish in Southeast Asia using this method has increased nearly 1,000 times since 1950. The Philippines and Indonesia join Taiwan as the top milkfish producers and consumers.

　　鹹粥是一種典型的台灣南部早餐，加上油條味道就很棒。做鹹粥的米要煮到軟且粒粒分明。就一般煮粥的方式，米會加大量的水煮足夠長的時間，使米粒軟到開始分解。台南鹹粥則是把清澈魚湯加在米飯上，在烹煮最後加入海鮮和蔬菜。鹹粥的主要成分是虱目魚，這是一種很受歡迎吃起來軟嫩的魚。在台南虱目魚的吃法還有許多方式，做湯、用煎的，或做成魚丸。在台灣吃的虱目魚大部分都不是野生捕撈的，而是由池塘養殖或養魚系統。傳統上，魚苗是在大海捕獲的，然後養在池塘或靠近沿海溫度較暖和的鹹水魚塭內。自 1950 年在東南亞用這種方法養殖虱目魚產量就增加了近 1000 倍。菲律賓和印尼加入台灣成為主要的虱目魚生產者和消費者。

　　此部分為**聽、讀雙效「填空」練習**，現在就一起動身，開始聽「短段落」，提升常考字彙、語感等答題能力！

　　1._____ porridge is a classic 2._____ Taiwan 3._____ dish, enjoyed with gusto – and a fried donut stick – in Tainan. The rice and broth for this salty porridge are prepared so that the 4._____ remains light and firm. In the 5._____ rice congee, the rice is cooked with large amounts of 6._____ long enough to make the 7._____ so soft that they begin to break apart. Salty porridge in Tainan is made so that the clear fish broth is added over the cooked rice, 8._____ and any 9._____ at the end of cooking. And the main 10._____ of salty porridge is milkfish – a 11._____, mild-tasting white fish. There are many other ways that milkfish is enjoyed in Tainan – in soup, fried, and as fish balls, for example. Most Milkfish 12._____ in Taiwan is not wild-caught, but raised through 13._____ or fish farming systems. Traditionally, the fish fingerlings are caught in the open 14._____, then raised in 15._____ or under-water cages of warm, brackish coastal water. Production of milkfish in Southeast 16._____ using this method has increased nearly 1,000 times since 1950. The 17._____ and 18._____ join Taiwan as the top milkfish 19._____ and 20._____.

▶▶ 參考答案

1. Salty	2. southern
3. breakfast	4. rice
5. common	6. water
7. grains	8. seafood
9. vegetables	10. ingredient
11. popular	12. available
13. aquaculture	14. sea
15. ponds	16. Asia
17. Philippines	18. Indonesia
19. producers	20. consumers

❶ Salty porridge is a classic southern Taiwan _____ dish, enjoyed with gusto – and a fried donut stick – in Tainan.

❷ The preparation process makes the rice _____ and _____.

❸ Plenty of _____ is needed to cook rice congee.

❹ At the end of cooking _____ and _____ will be added.

❺ Cooking methods of the Milkfish: in soup, fried, and as _____.

❻ Most Milkfish available in Taiwan is not _____.

❼ The fish fingerlings are bred in _____ after getting captured.

❽ _____ and _____ join Taiwan as the top milkfish producers and consumers.

❶ breakfast

❷ light, firm

❸ water

❹ seafood, vegetables

❺ fish balls

❻ wild-caught

❼ ponds

❽ The Philippines, Indonesia

台南－土產牛肉

Tainan Local Beef

▶▶ 影子跟讀「短段落」練習 🎧 MP3 003

　　此篇為「影子跟讀短段落練習」，規劃了由聽「短段落」的 shadowing 練習，強化聽力專注力和掌握各個考點！

　　Tainan's famous beef soup is a clear beef broth with Chinese herbs, poured boiling hot over raw pieces of thinly sliced beef. The heat of the soup cooks the beef as the vendor serves it. The best beef soup to be found on Tainan's streets uses local beef that comes fresh daily from the beef cattle farms near Tainan. Butchering occurs twice a day, once in the morning and once at night, in Shan Hua Tainan. This allows for the freshly butchered beef to be delivered directly to soup shops in the heart of the city and served as fresh as possible. Unlike western beef that is frozen right after butchering, Shan Hua Cattle Market provides "body temperature beef" which is cut beef that involves no freezing process and the meat structural integrity is not destroyed. Beef is cut and soon delivered to the market. It is said that only "body temperature beef" can be used for the best result for Tainan beef soup. Beef farming is not a large industry in Taiwan and the domestic beef is exclusively for local restaurants.

Beef is becoming more available for household cooking with French retailer Carefour and American retailer Costco selling their beef imported from Australia or the US.

　　台南著名的牛肉湯湯頭是中藥熬煮的清湯，滾燙的清湯，再倒入切得超薄的牛肉就可以上桌了。湯頭的熱度在上桌的同時會把牛肉幾乎燙熟。在台南最好的牛肉湯，是用每天來自台南附近養殖場的本地牛肉。台南善化牛墟，一天屠宰牛隻兩次，分別在上午和晚上，這樣可以讓新鮮屠宰的牛肉被直接送至各城市的小吃店，小吃店所提供的牛肉也就越新鮮越好。不像西方牛肉通常是在屠宰後立即冷凍，善化牛墟提供的是「溫體牛」，就是現殺，沒經過冷藏，肉質結構完整沒被破壞的，溫體牛在屠宰後很快就被供應到市場。有人說，只有「體溫牛」才能做出最棒的台南牛肉湯。牛肉養殖在台灣不是一個大產業，國內的牛肉是專門賣給小吃店。來自法國大賣場的家樂福和美國大賣場的好市多所賣的牛肉是澳大利亞和美國進口的，這樣一般家庭就比較容易買到牛肉。

　　此部分為**聽、讀雙效「填空」練習**，現在就一起動身，開始聽「短段落」，提升常考字彙、語感等答題能力！

　　Tainan's 1.＿＿＿＿＿＿＿ beef soup is a clear beef broth with Chinese 2.＿＿＿＿＿＿＿, poured boiling hot over raw pieces of thinly sliced beef. The 3.＿＿＿＿＿＿＿ of the soup cooks the beef as the 4.＿＿＿＿＿＿＿ serves it. The best beef soup to be found on Tainan's streets uses 5.＿＿＿＿＿＿＿ beef that comes 6.＿＿＿＿＿＿＿ daily from the beef 7.＿＿＿＿＿＿＿ farms near Tainan. 8.＿＿＿＿＿＿＿ occurs twice a day, once in the morning and once at night, in Shan Hua Tainan. This allows for the freshly butchered beef to be 9.＿＿＿＿＿＿＿ directly to soup shops in the 10.＿＿＿＿＿＿＿ of the city and served as fresh as possible. Unlike western beef that is 11.＿＿＿＿＿＿＿ right after butchering, Shan Hua Cattle Market provides "body 12.＿＿＿＿＿＿＿ beef" which is cut beef that involves no 13.＿＿＿＿＿＿＿ process and the meat structural 14.＿＿＿＿＿＿＿ is not destroyed. Beef is cut and soon delivered to the market. It is said that only "body temperature beef" can be used for the best result for Tainan beef soup. Beef farming is not a large 15.＿＿＿＿＿＿＿ in Taiwan and the 16.＿＿＿＿＿＿＿ beef is 17.＿＿＿＿＿＿＿ for local restaurants. Beef is becoming more 18.＿＿＿＿＿＿＿ for 19.＿＿＿＿＿＿＿ cooking with 20.＿＿＿＿＿＿＿ retailer Carefour and American retailer Costco selling their beef imported from Australia or the US.

▶▶ 參考答案

1. famous	2. herbs
3. heat	4. vendor
5. local	6. fresh
7. cattle	8. Butchering
9. delivered	10. heart
11. frozen	12. temperature
13. freezing	14. integrity
15. industry	16. domestic
17. exclusively	18. available
19. household	20. French

❶ Tainan's famous beef soup is a clear beef broth with Chinese _____, poured boiling hot over raw pieces of thinly sliced beef.

❷ Frequency of butchering: _____.

❸ _____ to the city soup shops can be maintained by the butchering ritual.

❹ Western beef remains _____ right after processing

❺ "Body temperature beef" which is able to maintain the _____ _____ of the meat structure.

❻ "Body temperature beef" will not include the _____ process.

❼ The domestic beef is exclusively for local _____.

❽ _____ and _____ retailers make beef accessible to every family.

❶ herbs

❷ twice

❸ Delivery

❹ frozen

❺ integrity

❻ freezing

❼ restaurants

❽ French, American

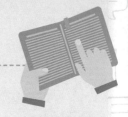

高雄－楊桃湯
Kaohsiung Star Fruit Drink

▶ 影子跟讀「短段落」練習 🎧 MP3 004

此篇為「**影子跟讀短段落練習**」，規劃了由聽「**短段落**」的 shadowing 練習，強化聽力專注力和掌握各個考點！

Star fruit – also known as carambola – is a sweet and juicy tropical fruit with five distinct ridges running its length. Carambola's roots, branches, leaves, flowers, and fruits all can be used for medicinal purposes. Carambola contains sucrose, fructose, glucose, malic acid, citric acid, oxalic acid and vitamins B1, B2, C and protein. In ancient times, it was used for its antibiotic effect to fight malaria. Star fruit in Taiwan is commonly used for sore throat. Turning the fruit into fermented juice is as simple as combining equal parts of sliced fruit and sugar in a large jar, covering it to keep the insects out, and setting the jar in the sun for a few days.

楊桃是一種五角形、甜美多汁的熱帶水果。楊桃的根、枝、葉、花、果都有藥用性質。楊桃含有蔗糖、果糖、葡萄糖、蘋果酸、檸檬酸、草酸、維生素 B1、B2、C 及蛋白質。在古代，楊桃的抗生素效果被用來對抗瘧疾。在台灣楊桃常用於治咽喉腫痛。楊桃汁是由發酵

過的楊桃所做的，發酵的楊桃做法很簡單，楊桃切片後每一層撒上糖放入一個大罐子，蓋起來防止害蟲入侵，放在太陽下幾天就完成了。

Alcohol content would increase to the level of a fruit wine if the jar was left for a full three weeks. Vendors serve up the fermented drink ice cold in plastic to-go cups with straws. Fermented star fruit drink can also be served hot. In addition to ready to serve cold star fruit drink, vendors also sell concentrated star fruit drink in bottles. In winter people like to add hot water to the concentrated star fruit drink.

如果放滿三星期，楊桃發酵後的酒精含量就能釀成水果酒。攤販賣的楊桃湯通常會把冰冷的楊桃湯倒入塑料外帶杯裝的吸管。楊桃湯也可以做熱飲。一般攤販除了賣馬上可以喝的冰楊桃湯，他們也會賣瓶裝的濃縮楊桃湯。冬天很多人喜歡買濃縮的楊桃湯回家自己加熱水。

　　此部分為**聽、讀雙效「填空」練習**，現在就一起動身，開始聽「短段落」，提升常考字彙、語感等答題能力！

　　Star1.＿＿＿＿＿＿＿ – also known as carambola – is a sweet and juicy 2.＿＿＿＿＿＿＿ fruit with five 3.＿＿＿＿＿＿＿ ridges running its 4.＿＿＿＿＿＿＿. Carambola's roots, 5.＿＿＿＿＿＿＿, leaves, 6.＿＿＿＿＿＿＿, and fruits all can be used for 7.＿＿＿＿＿＿＿ purposes. Carambola contains sucrose, fructose, 8.＿＿＿＿＿＿＿, malic acid, citric acid, oxalic acid and 9.＿＿＿＿＿＿＿ B1, B2, C and protein. In ancient times, it was used for its 10.＿＿＿＿＿＿＿ effect to fight 11.＿＿＿＿＿＿＿. Star fruit in Taiwan is commonly used for sore 12.＿＿＿＿＿＿＿. Turning the fruit into 13.＿＿＿＿＿＿＿ juice is as simple as combining equal parts of sliced fruit and 14.＿＿＿＿＿＿＿ in a large jar, covering it to keep the 15.＿＿＿＿＿＿＿ out, and setting the jar in the 16.＿＿＿＿＿＿＿ for a few days. Alcohol 17.＿＿＿＿＿＿＿ would increase to the level of a fruit 18.＿＿＿＿＿＿＿ if the jar was left for a full three weeks. Vendors serve up the fermented drink 19.＿＿＿＿＿＿＿ cold in plastic to-go cups with 20.＿＿＿＿＿＿＿. Fermented star fruit drink can also be served hot. In addition to ready to serve cold star fruit drink, vendors also sell concentrated star fruit drink in bottles. In winter people like to add hot water to the concentrated star fruit drink.

▶▶ 參考答案

1. fruit	2. tropical
3. distinct	4. length
5. branches	6. flowers
7. medicinal	8. glucose
9. vitamins	10. antibiotic
11. malaria	12. throat
13. fermented	14. sugar
15. insects	16. sun
17. content	18. wine
19. ice	20. straws

Part 1 生活類主題

Part 2 學術類主題

❶ Appearance: _____ distinct ridges

❷ purpose: _____ properties.

❸ In ancient times: could be used to fight against _____
___.

❹ nowadays: can be used to fight against _____.

❺ fermented juice: sliced fruit and _____ will be added.

❻ The jar will keep the _____ from entering it.

❼ a fruit wine: should be kept for _____ weeks.

❽ Fermented star fruit drink: can be served both hot and _____
_____.

❶ five

❷ medicinal

❸ malaria

❹ sore throat

❺ sugar

❻ insects

❼ three

❽ cold

高雄－鹹水鴨
Kaohsiung Salted Duck

▶▶ 影子跟讀「短段落」練習 🎧 MP3 005

此篇為「**影子跟讀短段落練習**」，規劃了由聽「**短段落**」的 shadowing 練習，強化聽力專注力和掌握各個考點！

Salted duck tastes effortless and simple, though the Kaohsiung cooks who prepare it have several steps to follow in order to make it well. The ingredients are simply duck, salt, pepper, ginger, green onion, and other spices. These are not hard to come by, so it is the various steps of marinating, cooking, and cooling that give the dish its traditional texture and taste. Traditional cooks may maintain the "starter broth" from previous salted duck cooking sessions to yield an even richer experience. Salted duck is a cold dish of sliced duck. Salted duck was originally a specialty of Nanjing, China, capital of the Qing Dynasty. The Qing emperor conquered and annexed Taiwan in the mid seventeenth century, ruling it for over two centuries. It's reasonable to assume that salted duck was brought to Taiwan from China. An amusing story from Nanjing attempts to explain how duck became so popular there centuries ago. Legend has it that a dispute about excess noise caused all the roosters to be killed. The result was no noisier wake-up calls, but also no more chicken to eat. This is said to be the time period when the locals turned to duck as a source of protein.

　　鹽水鴨吃起來是那麼輕鬆和簡單的味道，雖然簡單但是還是需要好幾個步驟才能做得出好吃的鹽水鴨。鹽水鴨的材料只是簡單的鴨、鹽、胡椒、薑、蔥和其他香料。這些材料都不難取得，透過醃製，烹調和冷卻的各個步驟，讓這道菜有很特別的傳統肉質和口感。有些廚師可能會保留煮過的鹽水鴨的高湯再加入煮新鹽水鴨，這樣可以讓味道更加豐富。鹽水鴨通常是切片的一道涼菜。鹽水鴨源自中國南京，是清朝首都的特產。清朝皇帝在十七世紀中期吞併台灣，統治了兩個多世紀。因此，可以合理的假設，台灣的鹽水鴨是源自中國。在南京有一個讓人莞爾一笑的說法，解釋為何鴨肉在那裡幾百年前這麼流行。傳說是過度噪音的糾紛導致所有的公雞被殺害。也因此早晨不會聽到吵醒居民的啼叫聲，但同時也沒有雞肉可以吃了。也就在那時，當地人把吃鴨肉作為蛋白質取得的來源。

此部分為**聽、讀雙效「填空」練習**，現在就一起動身，開始聽「短段落」，提升常考字彙、語感等答題能力！

Salted duck tastes 1.＿＿＿＿＿＿ and simple, though the Kaohsiung cooks who prepare it have 2.＿＿＿＿＿＿ steps to follow in order to make it well. The 3.＿＿＿＿＿＿ are simply 4.＿＿＿＿＿＿, salt, pepper, ginger, green 5.＿＿＿＿＿＿, and other spices. These are not hard to come by, so it is the various steps of 6.＿＿＿＿＿＿, cooking, and cooling that give the dish its traditional 7.＿＿＿＿＿＿ and taste. Traditional cooks may maintain the "starter broth" from previous salted duck cooking sessions to 8.＿＿＿＿＿＿ an even richer 9.＿＿＿＿＿＿. Salted duck is a cold dish of sliced duck. Salted duck was originally a 10.＿＿＿＿＿＿ of Nanjing, China, capital of the Qing 11.＿＿＿＿＿＿. The Qing 12.＿＿＿＿＿＿ conquered and annexed Taiwan in the mid seventeenth century, ruling it for over 13.＿＿＿＿＿＿ centuries. It's reasonable to assume that salted duck was brought to Taiwan from China. An amusing 14.＿＿＿＿＿＿ from Nanjing attempts to explain how duck became so popular there centuries ago. Legend has it that a 15.＿＿＿＿＿＿ about excess 16.＿＿＿＿＿＿ caused all the 17.＿＿＿＿＿＿ to be killed. The result was no noisier wake-up calls, but also no more 18.＿＿＿＿＿＿ to eat. This is said to be the time period when the 19.＿＿＿＿＿＿ turned to duck as a source of 20.＿＿＿＿＿＿.

▶▶ 參考答案

1. effortless	2. several
3. ingredients	4. duck
5. onion	6. marinating
7. texture	8. yield
9. experience	10. specialty
11. Dynasty	12. emperor
13. two	14. story
15. dispute	16. noise
17. roosters	18. chicken
19. locals	20. protein

❶ ingredients: duck, salt, _____, _____, green onion, and other spices.

❷ steps: _____, cooking, and cooling.

❸ Salted duck is a _____ dish of sliced duck.

❹ origin: _____

❺ in the mid seventeenth century: The Qing _____ conquered and annexed Taiwan

❻ story: an explanation of why duck became _____.

❼ dispute: _____ were killed due to the noise.

❽ Duck became the replacement because of its _____.

Part 1 生活類主題

Part 2 學術類主題

❶ pepper, ginger

❷ marinating

❸ cold

❹ China

❺ emperor

❻ popular

❼ roosters

❽ protein

屏東－東港鮪魚

Pingtung Dong Gang Tuna

▶▶ 影子跟讀「短段落」練習 🎧 MP3 006

此篇為「影子跟讀短段落練習」，規劃了由聽「短段落」的 shadowing 練習，強化聽力專注力和掌握各個考點！

There is no better time to go to Dong Gang port in Pingtung than during the annual Blue Fin Tuna Cultural Festival. Every year from May to July, the visitor can find a major celebration of tuna, founded securely in Pingtung's coastal Dong Gang Township in this tropical, southern area of Taiwan. Pacific blue fin tuna is much sought after, especially in Taiwan and Japan, for high quality sushi and sashimi. The Taiwanese tuna catch used to go almost exclusively to Japan, where bidders still pay top dollar for the rights to serve the biggest and best of the catch. Now, "tuna fever" captures the entire island of Taiwan during the later spring and early summer timeframe. In Taiwan, blue fin tuna is often referred to as "black tuna," but it is the same fish. Sakura shrimp and salted oilfish eggs are also popular in Dong Gang. The growth period for Sakura shrimp runs from November to June in the nearby coastal waters of Dong Gang port. Sakura shrimp has red pigment and light-emitting organs. It is usually fried or dried. Oilfish's eggs are salted, pressed and dried. It is usually thin sliced and is eaten with garlic and raw white radish.

　　東港黑鮪魚文化觀光季是去屏東東港的好時機。每年 5 月至 7 月，在台灣這個熱帶南部地區的屏東沿海東港鎮遊客可以看到有關黑鮪魚主要慶祝活動。太平洋黑鮪魚有很高的市場需求，特別是在台灣和日本，因為可以用來做高品質的壽司和生魚片。台灣以前捕獲的鮪魚幾乎都是賣去日本，投標人會付最高的價錢來買到最大和最好的魚。「黑鮪魚熱潮」現在則在春季和初夏時間風靡台灣。在台灣，這樣的藍鰭金槍魚常常被稱為「黑鮪魚」。東港還有櫻花蝦、油魚子。櫻花蝦產期為每年 11 至翌年 6 月就在東港溪出海口附近。櫻花蝦全身佈滿紅色素及發光器，通常會乾製或炸酥。油魚子的卵鹽醃後晾乾，吃的時候切成薄片再配上蒜苗與白蘿蔔。

此部分為**聽、讀雙效「填空」練習**，現在就一起動身，開始聽「短段落」，提升常考字彙、語感等答題能力！

There is no better time to go to Dong Gang port in Pingtung than during the annual 1._____ Fin Tuna Cultural Festival. Every year from 2._____ to 3._____, the visitor can find a major 4._____ of tuna, founded securely in Pingtung's 5._____ Dong Gang Township in this tropical, southern area of Taiwan. Pacific blue fin tuna is much sought after, 6._____ in Taiwan and 7._____, for high quality sushi and sashimi. The Taiwanese tuna 8._____ used to go almost 9._____ to Japan, where 10._____ still pay top 11._____ for the rights to serve the biggest and best of the catch. Now, "tuna fever" captures the entire 12._____ of Taiwan during the later spring and early 13._____ timeframe. In Taiwan, blue fin tuna is often referred to as "14._____ tuna," but it is the same fish. Sakura shrimp and salted oilfish 15._____ are also popular in Dong Gang. The 16._____ period for Sakura shrimp runs from 17._____ to 18._____ in the nearby coastal waters of Dong Gang port. Sakura shrimp has 19._____ pigment and light-emitting 20._____. It is usually fried or dried. Oilfish's eggs are salted, pressed and dried. It is usually thin sliced and is eaten with garlic and raw white radish.

▶▶ 參考答案

1. Blue	2. May
3. July	4. celebration
5. coastal	6. especially
7. Japan	8. catch
9. exclusively	10. bidders
11. dollar	12. island
13. summer	14. black
15. eggs	16. growth
17. November	18. June
19. red	20. organs

❶ Time: from _____ to _____

❷ dish of the blue fin tuna: _____ and _____

❸ sale of the captured tuna: _____

❹ the rights: _____ will pay plenty.

❺ timeframe of the tuna fever: _____ and _____
_____

❻ another name for blue fin tuna: _____

❼ other popular items in Dong Gang: Sakura _____ and salted oilfish _____

❽ pigment of the Sakura shrimp: _____

❶ May, July

❷ sushi, sashimi

❸ Japan

❹ bidders

❺ spring, summer

❻ black tuna

❼ shrimp, eggs

❽ red

UNIT 7

屏東－潮州旗魚黑輪
Pintung-Oo-lián, Fishcakes, Oolen, Tian Bu La

▶▶ 影子跟讀「短段落」練習 🎧 MP3 007

此篇為「**影子跟讀短段落練習**」，規劃了由聽「**短段落**」的 shadowing 練習，強化聽力專注力和掌握各個考點！

Fish cake or oolen/tian bu la is a savory fried fish cake, primarily made of a paste of various types of seafood, potato starch, sugar, and pepper. The ingredients are ground and mashed into a smooth mixture, then shaped into a log for frying. The result is a springy, slightly chewy texture – that "Q" that is so important and popular in Taiwanese cuisine. Normally, the fried fish cake is served on a stick with a sweet and sour sauce. These fried fish cakes, along with fish balls and other delicacies are also available floating in a soup – inspired by the Japanese, as are fish cakes themselves. Pintung County, on the southernmost tip of Taiwan, is home to beautiful natural parks, seaports, and unique coral beaches. It is also the location where, in 1874, the Japanese landed and won bloody victories against the local tribes. This was the beginning of a twenty-year war for the island, won ultimately by the Japanese. This early battle is memorialized at the historic site ShiMen Ancient Battlefield. Though the site's memorials are somber, the mountainous landscape is breath-taking. Beautiful temples, artist colonies, tribal grounds and many other fascinating attractions are available throughout Pintung.

　　黑輪是一種用魚漿做的美味油炸小吃，主要由各類海鮮、馬鈴薯澱粉、糖和胡椒粉所做。把混合均勻的麵糊做成長條狀後再油炸。這樣做出來的黑輪就是很有彈性、耐嚼感，也就是大家喜歡的台灣美食的「Q」感。黑輪的吃法是串在竹子上，加上甜酸醬。通常是煮一大鍋黑輪，搭配魚丸和其他食材，這種靈感來自於日本人的小吃。屏東縣位在台灣的最南端，這裡有美麗的自然公園、海港和獨特的珊瑚海灘。這裡也是 1874 年日本軍隊抵達後與當地部落作戰的地方。原住民在這個島嶼與日本人對抗二十多年的戰爭，最後由日本人戰勝。這個早期的戰鬥歷史的紀念遺址就是現在的石門古戰場。雖然紀念史蹟是嚴肅的，這裡的山區景觀卻是讓人驚歎。整個屏東地方都可以看到美麗的寺廟、藝術家集聚、部落地方和其他許多迷人丰采的景觀。

此部分為**聽、讀雙效「填空」練習**，現在就一起動身，開始聽「短段落」，提升常考字彙、語感等答題能力！

Fish cake or oolen/tian bu la is a savory fried fish 1._____, primarily made of a paste of various types of 2._____, potato 3._____, sugar, and 4._____. The ingredients are ground and mashed into a smooth 5._____, then shaped into a log for frying. The result is a springy, slightly chewy texture – that "Q" that is so important and popular in Taiwanese 5._____. Normally, the fried fish cake is served on a 6._____ with a sweet and sour sauce. These fried fish cakes, along with fish balls and other delicacies are also 7._____ floating in a soup – inspired by the 8._____, as are fish cakes themselves. Pintung County, on the southernmost tip of Taiwan, is home to 9._____ natural parks, 10._____, and unique 11._____ beaches. It is also the 12._____ where, in 13._____, the Japanese landed and won bloody 14._____ against the local tribes. This was the beginning of a twenty-year war for the island, won ultimately by the Japanese. This early battle is memorialized at the 15._____ site ShiMen Ancient Battlefield. Though the site's memorials are somber, the mountainous 16._____ is breath-taking. Beautiful 17._____, artist colonies, tribal grounds and many other fascinating 18._____ are available throughout Pintung.

▶▶ 參考答案

1. cake	2. seafood
3. starch	4. pepper
5. mixture	6. stick
7. available	8. Japanese
9. beautiful	10. seaports
11. coral	12. location
13. 1874	14. victories
15. historic	16. landscape
17. temples	18. attractions

❶ ingredients: _____, potato starch, _____, and pepper

❷ shape: a _____ for frying

❸ texture: springy, slightly _____

❹ eating: the fried fish cake is served on a _____

❺ inspiration: from the _____

❻ geography: natural parks, _____, and unique coral __ _____

❼ time of the battle: _____

❽ landscape: Beautiful _____, artist _____, tribal grounds

❶ seafood, sugar

❷ log

❸ chewy

❹ stick

❺ Japanese

❻ seaports, beaches

❼ 1874

❽ temples, colonies

宜蘭－三星蔥油餅
Onion Scallion Flatbread

▶▶ 影子跟讀「短段落」練習 🎧 MP3 008

此篇為「影子跟讀短段落練習」，規劃了由聽「短段落」的 shadowing 練習，強化聽力專注力和掌握各個考點！

One well-known and well-loved finger food in Taiwan is scallion flatbread. It uses such simple ingredients and preparation, though the result is so tasty! The cook prepares a basic wheat flour and water dough, rolls a large piece out to add oil, diced scallions and salt, then rolls small pieces into circles for pan-frying into flaky finger food. In Ilan and other areas of Taiwan, street vendors offer either plain or in a classic Taiwanese style with an egg. This treat arrived in Taiwan from mainland China when the imperial army and its supporters fled during the communist takeover. The origin of scallion flatbread – or sometimes called fried green onion pancake – is not specifically known. Some sources suppose that the Indian population of Beijing may have had a hand in developing this Chinese treat, since it is similar to a flatbread they loved from their cuisine, called paratha. Ilan county in the northeast coastal area of Taiwan was home to two aboriginal groups: a mountain settlement of Atayal people and a coastal and riverbank group of settlements by the Kavalan, after which the county is named. The best scallion flatbread is from Ilan where it grows the best green onion called Sansing Green Onion.

　　蔥油餅是眾所皆知且深受大家喜愛的台灣小吃。雖然只是簡單的材料和做法，但就是非常好吃！做法是用基本的小麥粉和水做成麵團再桿成一大塊，在麵皮上加油、香蔥和鹽，捲成圓形狀，要煎之前再桿開好下鍋油煎，這就是有層次的蔥油餅。在宜蘭及台灣等地區，街頭攤販會賣一般或加蛋的蔥油餅。這種小吃是當時國民黨在大陸撤退逃離到台灣時所帶進來的小吃。蔥油餅或蔥花大餅並沒有考據的來源。有些來源指出在北京的印度人口對這個在中國的小吃有啟發的影響，因為這與印度人自己的印度大餅很類似。在台灣東北部沿海地區的宜蘭縣是兩個當地原住民：一是靠山的泰雅族人和沿海河岸而居的噶瑪蘭人，這也是宜蘭縣被命名的起源。最好的蔥油餅在宜蘭，因為這裡所生長的三星蔥是最棒的蔥。

　　此部分為**聽、讀雙效「填空」練習**，現在就一起動身，開始聽「短段落」，提升常考字彙、語感等答題能力！

　　One well-known and well-loved finger food in Taiwan is scallion flatbread. It uses such 1.＿＿＿＿＿＿＿ ingredients and 2.＿＿＿＿＿＿＿, though the 3.＿＿＿＿＿＿＿ is so tasty! The cook prepares a 4.＿＿＿＿＿＿＿ wheat flour and water 5.＿＿＿＿＿＿＿, rolls a large piece out to add 6.＿＿＿＿＿＿＿, diced scallions and salt, then rolls 7.＿＿＿＿＿＿＿ pieces into 8.＿＿＿＿＿＿＿ for pan-frying into flaky finger food. In Ilan and other areas of Taiwan, street vendors offer either 9.＿＿＿＿＿＿＿ or in a 10.＿＿＿＿＿＿＿ Taiwanese style with an egg. This treat arrived in Taiwan from 11.＿＿＿＿＿＿＿ China when the imperial army and its 12.＿＿＿＿＿＿＿ fled during the 13.＿＿＿＿＿＿＿ takeover. The origin of scallion flatbread – or sometimes called fried green onion pancake – is not 14.＿＿＿＿＿＿＿ known. Some 15.＿＿＿＿＿＿＿ suppose that the Indian population of Beijing may have had a hand in developing this Chinese treat, since it is 16.＿＿＿＿＿＿＿ to a flatbread they loved from their cuisine, called paratha. Ilan county in the northeast coastal area of Taiwan was home to two 17.＿＿＿＿＿＿＿ groups: a mountain 18.＿＿＿＿＿＿＿ of Atayal people and a coastal and 19.＿＿＿＿＿＿＿ group of 20.＿＿＿＿＿＿＿ by the Kavalan, after which the county is named. The best scallion flatbread is from Ilan where it grows the best green onion called Sansing Green Onion.

▶▶ 參考答案

1. simple	2. preparation
3. result	4. basic
5. dough	6. oil
7. small	8. circles
9. plain	10. classic
11. mainland	12. supporters
13. communist	14. specifically
15. sources	16. similar
17. aboriginal	18. settlement
19. riverbank	20. settlements

❶ preparation: wheat _____ and water _____

❷ sprinkle: scallions and _____

❸ cooking: scallion flatbread with an _____

❹ another name for scallion flatbread: fried _____ onion pancake

❺ inspiration: the _____ population

❻ paratha: a _____

❼ settlement of Atayal people: _____

❽ settlements by the Kavalan: a coastal and _____ group

❶ flour, dough

❷ salt

❸ egg

❹ green

❺ Indian

❻ flatbread

❼ mountain

❽ riverbank

宜蘭－魚丸米粉

Ilan-Fish Ball and Rice Noodle Soup

▶▶ **影子跟讀「短段落」練習** 🎧 MP3 009

此篇為「**影子跟讀短段落練習**」，規劃了由聽「**短段落**」的 shadowing 練習，強化聽力專注力和掌握各個考點！

Tofu (or Dou Fu) and other soy products like fresh or frozen green soybeans for eating, soy sauce and soy milk are important staples in Taiwanese kitchens and plentiful in street vendors' stalls. Taiwan is within the top 10 countries in soybean consumption in the world. Almost 10 percent of Taiwan's arable land is planted to soybeans, yet 97 percent of the soy Taiwan needs is imported from other countries. In fact, US soybeans make up 55 percent of what Taiwan imports of this high protein snack, condiment or main dish. Small scale manufacturers still make bean curd by hand and deliver it to markets and restaurants every morning. The process for making bean curd involves soaking soy beans, grinding them, straining off the soy milk, then coagulating what is left before placing the semi-solid remainder into a mold so that it can "set." Once tofu is made, it is eatable. It can also be made into different products. Oily tofu is fried tofu, which is popularly added in soups or hot pot in Taiwan. Fried tofu is a key ingredient in making an authentic bowl of fish and noodle soup in Ilan.

豆腐或其他豆製品如用來吃的新鮮或冷凍毛豆、醬油和豆漿都是在台灣的家庭或路邊攤烹煮的重要食材。台灣是全世界消費黃豆排名前 10 名的國家。台灣的耕地有近 10%是種植黃豆，而台灣所需要的黃豆有 97%是從其他國家進口的。事實上，美國的黃豆佔台灣進口量的 55%，黃豆是高蛋白的來源，也可做調味品或主菜。小規模的豆腐生產廠家還是有人用手工做豆腐，每天早晨提供給市場和餐館。豆腐的製作方法包括浸泡大豆，研磨，過濾豆漿，凝固後把半成品放入模型「成型」。一旦豆腐做好了，可以馬上食用，也可以做成不同產品。油豆腐可以放入湯或火鍋，在台灣這都是流行的吃法。油豆腐是宜蘭魚丸米粉的一個關鍵食材。

　　此部分為**聽、讀雙效「填空」練習**，現在就一起動身，開始聽「短段落」，提升常考字彙、語感等答題能力！

　　Tofu (or Dou Fu) and other soy 1.＿＿＿＿＿＿＿ like fresh or frozen 2.＿＿＿＿＿＿＿ soybeans for eating, soy sauce and soy milk are important 3.＿＿＿＿＿＿＿ in Taiwanese 4.＿＿＿＿＿＿＿ and 5.＿＿＿＿＿＿＿ in street vendors' stalls. Taiwan is within the top 10 countries in soybean 6.＿＿＿＿＿＿＿ in the world. Almost 10 7.＿＿＿＿＿＿＿ of Taiwan's 8.＿＿＿＿＿＿＿ land is planted to soybeans, yet 9.＿＿＿＿＿＿＿ percent of the soy Taiwan needs is 10.＿＿＿＿＿＿＿ from other countries. In fact, US soybeans make up 11.＿＿＿＿＿＿＿ percent of what Taiwan imports of this high 12.＿＿＿＿＿＿＿ snack, condiment or main dish. Small scale 13.＿＿＿＿＿＿＿ still make bean curd by hand and deliver it to markets and 14.＿＿＿＿＿＿＿ every morning. The 15.＿＿＿＿＿＿＿ for making bean curd involves soaking soy beans, grinding them, straining off the soy 16.＿＿＿＿＿＿＿, then coagulating what is left before placing the semi-solid 17.＿＿＿＿＿＿＿ into a mold so that it can "set." Once tofu is made, it is 18.＿＿＿＿＿＿＿. It can also be made into different products. Oily tofu is fried tofu, which is 19.＿＿＿＿＿＿＿ added in soups or hot pot in Taiwan. Fried tofu is a key ingredient in making an authentic 20.＿＿＿＿＿＿＿ of fish and noodle soup in Ilan.

▶▶ 參考答案

1. products
2. green
3. staples
4. kitchens
5. plentiful
6. consumption
7. percent
8. arable
9. 97
10. imported
11. 55
12. protein
13. manufacturers
14. restaurants
15. process
16. milk
17. remainder
18. eatable
19. popularly
20. bowl

❶ staples: green soybeans for eating, soy sauce and soy _____
  _____

❷ soybean consumption: top 10 _____

❸ arable land planting soybeans: almost _____ percent

❹ imported: _____ percent

❺ US soybeans: _____ percent

❻ Small scale manufacturers: make bean curd by _____
  __

❼ process: soaking, _____, and straining

❽ an authentic bowl of fish and noodle soup: includes _____
  _____

❶ milk

❷ countries

❸ 10

❹ 97

❺ 55

❻ hand

❼ grinding

❽ fried tofu

UNIT ⑩

嘉義－豆花
Chiayi Tofu Pudding, Doufu Hua, Douhua

▶▶ 影子跟讀「短段落」練習 🎧 MP3 010

此篇為「**影子跟讀短段落練習**」，規劃了由聽「**短段落**」的 shadowing 練習，強化聽力專注力和掌握各個考點！

Tofu pudding, doufu hua, douhua, or translated directly "tofu flower" is a simple, traditional dessert, forms of which you can find around East Asia. The Taiwan form can be cold in summer or warm in winter, but always refreshing. Rolling carts of soy milk vendors were common in earlier days, bringing their product into neighborhoods and making all the kids beg their mothers for a little money to buy this treat. It is simply soy milk made fresh daily into a gelatin-like form, floating in a thin brown sugar syrup and topped with sweetened black beans, red beans, or peanuts. In other parts of Asia, there might be ginger or almond in the syrup, or it may also be savory and served for breakfast. It is possible to find these forms of tofu pudding also in Taiwan, but the most traditional is simply topped with sugar syrup. Chiayi county has a strong, diverse economy with lumber from the Ali mountains in the west, central location for strong transportation and communication sectors, plus strong industry and educational institutions. Chiayi hosts a famous international music festival during the last two weeks of December, providing performance and learning opportunities for participants from across the globe.

　　豆腐布丁、豆腐花、豆花，或直接翻譯成「豆花」其實就是一個簡單的、傳統的甜點，這在東南亞很普遍。台灣的豆花在夏天是吃冷的，在冬天是吃溫的，兩種吃法都會讓人很驚喜。在早期流動豆漿攤販是很常見的，他們在社區裡賣豆花，很多孩子就會向媽媽討一點錢來買這種甜點。這其實是豆漿做成有膠狀的甜點，在上面淋上黑糖漿加上甜黑豆、紅豆或花生。在亞洲其他地區，有些地方會加薑或杏仁的糖漿，或是做成鹹的，或者也有人當早餐吃。在台灣這種口味的豆花也很普遍，但真正傳統的口味只是淋上糖漿。嘉義縣因為有阿里山山脈生產木材而有強大也多樣化的經濟與運輸和通信行業，也有很不錯的產業和教育機構。嘉義在 12 月的最後兩個星期會舉辦來自世界各地的國際著名音樂節，提供參加者表演和學習的機會。

此部分為**聽、讀雙效「填空」練習**,現在就一起動身,開始聽「短段落」,提升常考字彙、語感等答題能力!

Tofu pudding, doufu hua, douhua, or 1._____ directly "tofu flower" is a simple, traditional 2._____, forms of which you can find around East Asia. The Taiwan form can be cold in 3._____ or warm in 4._____, but always refreshing. Rolling 5._____ of soy milk vendors were common in earlier days, bringing their 6._____ into 7._____ and making all the kids beg their mothers for a little 8._____ to buy this treat. It is simply soy milk made 9._____ daily into a gelatin-like form, floating in a thin 10._____ sugar syrup and topped with sweetened 11._____ beans, red beans, or 12._____. In other parts of Asia, there might be ginger or 13._____ in the syrup, or it may also be 14._____ and served for 15._____. It is possible to find these forms of tofu pudding also in Taiwan, but the most traditional is simply topped with sugar syrup. Chiayi county has a strong, diverse 16._____ with 17._____ from the Ali 18._____ in the west, central location for strong transportation and 19._____ sectors, plus strong industry and educational institutions. Chiayi hosts a famous international music festival during the last two weeks of 20._____, providing performance and learning opportunities for participants from across the globe.

▶▶ 參考答案

1. translated	2. dessert
3. summer	4. winter
5. carts	6. product
7. neighborhoods	8. money
9. fresh	10. brown
11. black	12. peanuts
13. almond	14. savory
15. breakfast	16. economy
17. lumber	18. mountains
19. communication	20. December

❶ direct translation: tofu _____

❷ in summer: it's served _____.

❸ vendors/earlier days: sold through rolling _____

❹ kids: beg _____ for this treat.

❺ floating: in a sugary _____

❻ other condiments: sweetened black beans, red beans, or _____
_____.

❼ Ali mountains: rich in _____.

❽ industry in Chiayi: _____ and _____ sectors

❶ flower

❷ cold

❸ carts

❹ money

❺ syrup

❻ peanuts

❼ lumber

❽ transportation, communication

雲林－炊仔飯
Yunlin Steamed Stuffed Rice

▶ 影子跟讀「短段落」練習 🎧 MP3 011

此篇為「**影子跟讀短段落練習**」，規劃了由聽「**短段落**」的 shadowing 練習，強化聽力專注力和掌握各個考點！

Tube rice, zhu tong fan, or bamboo rice is a traditional food of indigenous Taiwanese people. This savory dish is made from sticky rice and numerous local ingredients, all cooked but then stuffed into a 20 cm (8 inch) long mature, green bamboo stalk, then sealed and steamed. Because of the steaming, the rice and ingredients are melded together in a sticky, delicious tower or served in an opened bamboo stalk. The bamboo stalk was an excellent container not only to cook this light meal, but also for early hunters and gatherers to carry some nourishment on their expeditions. Primary ingredients are pork – or wild boar – shitake mushrooms, shallots and shrimp. Street vendors serve it with a delicious sauce and may top it with peanuts, pork thread or cilantro. Steamed stuffed rice is a similar dish using small bowls rather than bamboo stalks. Steamed stuffed rice originated in Yunlin and only can be found in Yunlin. Different from sticky rice used in tube rice, steamed stuffed rice uses regular cooked rice, stuffed with meat sauce and green peas into a small bowl then steamed. Tube rice can be found all over the island but steamed stuffed rice can only be found in Yunlin.

　　竹筒飯是台灣原住民的傳統食品。這種美味的菜餚是由糯米和當地食材煮熟後，放入 20 公分（八吋）的綠竹筒密封好後再蒸熟。因為有蒸過，因此所有的材料會混合在一起，煮好時切開來就可直接食用。竹筒是一種很棒的食材容器，不但能用來煮輕食，早期獵人打獵時也用來盛裝他們的食物。竹筒飯主要成分是野豬肉、香菇、紅蔥和蝦。有些小販會加上美味的醬料和花生、肉鬆或香菜。炊仔飯也是一種類似竹筒飯的美食，是用碗當蒸具而不是竹筒。炊仔飯起源於雲林，也只有在雲林才有。不同於竹筒飯裡所用的糯米，炊仔飯是用一般的米飯，將肉燥、青豆等配料都放到碗裡後再蒸熟。竹筒飯在台灣全島都可以吃的到，但是炊仔飯只有在雲林才有。

此部分為**聽、讀雙效「填空」練習**，現在就一起動身，開始聽「短段落」，提升常考字彙、語感等答題能力！

Tube rice, zhu tong fan, or bamboo rice is a traditional food of 1.＿＿＿＿＿＿ Taiwanese people. This savory dish is made from sticky rice and 2.＿＿＿＿＿＿ local ingredients, all cooked but then stuffed into a 20 cm (8 inch) long 3.＿＿＿＿＿＿, green 4.＿＿＿＿＿＿ stalk, then sealed and steamed. Because of the steaming, the 5.＿＿＿＿＿＿ and ingredients are melded together in a sticky, 6.＿＿＿＿＿＿ tower or served in an opened bamboo stalk. The bamboo stalk was an excellent 7.＿＿＿＿＿＿ not only to cook this 8.＿＿＿＿＿＿ meal, but also for early 9.＿＿＿＿＿＿ and gatherers to carry some 10.＿＿＿＿＿＿ on their 11.＿＿＿＿＿＿. Primary ingredients are 12.＿＿＿＿＿＿ – or wild boar – shitake 13.＿＿＿＿＿＿, shallots and shrimp. Street vendors serve it with a delicious 14.＿＿＿＿＿＿ and may top it with peanuts, pork thread or 15.＿＿＿＿＿＿. Steamed stuffed rice is a similar dish using small bowls rather than bamboo stalks. Steamed stuffed rice 16.＿＿＿＿＿＿ in Yunlin and only can be found in Yunlin. Different from sticky rice used in tube rice, steamed stuffed rice uses 17.＿＿＿＿＿＿ cooked rice, stuffed with meat sauce and 18.＿＿＿＿＿＿ peas into a small bowl then steamed. Tube rice can be found all over the island but steamed stuffed rice can only be found in Yunlin.

▶▶ **參考答案**

1. indigenous	2. numerous
3. mature	4. bamboo
5. rice	6. delicious
7. container	8. light
9. hunters	10. nourishment
11. expeditions	12. pork
13. mushrooms	14. sauce
15. cilantro	16. originated
17. regular	18. green

❶ savory dish: a mixture of _____ and numerous local ingredients

❷ length of the bamboo stalk: _____ cm

❸ function of the bamboo stalk: an excellent _____

❹ for hunters and gathers: _____ during their expeditions

❺ ingredients: pork – or wild boar – shitake mushrooms, _____ _____ and _____ .

❻ Street vendors: use additional condiments, such as peanuts, pork thread or _____

❼ Steamed stuffed rice: use _____ instead of bamboo

❽ tube rice: condiments will not be put in a container and _____ _____

1 sticky rice

2 20

3 container

4 nourishment

5 shallots, shrimp

6 cilantro

7 bowls

8 steam

東海－雞腳凍
Taichung Cold Chicken Feet

▶▶ 影子跟讀「短段落」練習 🎧 MP3 012

此篇為「**影子跟讀短段落練習**」，規劃了由聽「**短段落**」的 shadowing 練習，強化聽力專注力和掌握各個考點！

Cold chicken feet. While the name may not be appealing to some western tastes, chicken feet are an important part of traditional cuisines all over the world. Nowhere are chicken feet more popular than Taiwan, Hong Kong, and China. In fact, poultry producers in the United States make significant profits exporting chicken feet to Asia. Over the past 20 years, occasional poultry import bans due to faltering trade agreement negotiations or fears of avian flu have restricted the flow of US chicken to Asia. Typically, when added together, Taiwan, Hong Kong, and China are the destination of almost 25 percent of the US' poultry exports – an indication of how important chicken feet really are in the culture. Chicken feet are a traditional dim sum treat, originating in the Cantonese region of China, making them a perfect dish to enjoy from a street vendor in Taiwan. In night markets in Taiwan, especially the most famous place to buy them in Taichung City, they are served cold. It's not normally a hot and spicy dish, instead relying on the richness of the gelatinous texture of the feet, the skin, and the cooking process.

　　雞腳凍。雖然這個名字可能不會吸引西方人的胃口，雞爪其實是世界各地傳統美食一個重要的食材。沒有其他地方的雞爪比台灣、香港和中國更受歡迎。事實上，美國家禽生產商出口到亞洲雞爪有獲得顯著的利潤。在過去的 20 年裡，有時因為搖擺不定的貿易協定談判或對禽流感的憂慮禁止家禽進口，而制約了美國雞肉在亞洲的流動。一般情況下，台灣、香港和中國的市場需求加起來占有美國禽肉出口 24％的量，這也顯示雞爪在這些文化裡的重要性。雞爪是廣式飲茶的小吃，源自於中國的廣東地區，後來成為台灣流行的美食。在台灣的夜市，最有名的雞腳凍是在台中的夜市，這是冷食的。雞腳凍通常不是辛辣的小吃，雞腳凍好吃的地方是在雞腳的凝膠質，這是雞腳的皮所滷出來的口感。

此部分為**聽、讀雙效「填空」練習**，現在就一起動身，開始聽「短段落」，提升常考字彙、語感等答題能力！

Cold chicken feet. While the name may not be 1._____ to some western tastes, chicken feet are an important part of traditional 2._____ all over the world. Nowhere are chicken feet more popular than Taiwan, Hong Kong, and China. In fact, 3._____ producers in the United States make 4._____ profits exporting chicken feet to 5._____. Over the past 20 years, occasional poultry import 6._____ due to faltering 7._____ agreement 8._____ or fears of avian 9._____ have restricted the flow of US chicken to Asia. Typically, when added together, Taiwan, Hong Kong, and 10._____ are the destination of almost 11._____ percent of the US' poultry exports – an 12._____ of how important chicken feet really are in the culture. Chicken feet are a traditional 13._____ sum treat, originating in the 14._____ region of China, making them a perfect dish to enjoy from a 15._____ vendor in Taiwan. In night markets in Taiwan, especially the most famous place to buy them in Taichung City, they are served cold. It's not 16._____ a hot and spicy dish, instead relying on the 17._____ of the 18._____ texture of the feet, the skin, and the cooking process.

▶▶ 參考答案

1. appealing	2. cuisines
3. poultry	4. significant
5. Asia	6. bans
7. trade	8. negotiations
9. flu	10. China
11. 25	12. indication
13. dim	14. Cantonese
15. street	16. normally
17. richness	18. gelatinous

Part 1 生活類主題

Part 2 學術類主題

❶ popularity: in _____, Hong Kong, and China

❷ importing chicken feet: _____

❸ American poultry producers: earn significant _____

❹ agreement related to the restriction: _____ agreement

❺ disease related to the restriction: _____

❻ 3 countries: _____ percent of the US' poultry exports

❼ origin: the _____ region of China

❽ texture of the feet: _____

1 Taiwan

2 Asia

3 profits

4 trade

5 avian flu

6 25

7 Cantonese

8 gelatinous

台中－豬血糕
Taichung Pig's Blood Rice Cake

▶▶ **影子跟讀「短段落」練習** 🎧 MP3 013

　　此篇為「**影子跟讀短段落練習**」，規劃了由聽「**短段落**」的 shadowing 練習，強化聽力專注力和掌握各個考點！

　　Pig's blood rice cake is served on a stick in many night markets in Taiwan. The name is perhaps a little too honest for some, but the ingredients and texture are not completely unfamiliar to anyone who eats sausage, especially traditional European forms like boudin from France. Firm, yet chewy is the best way to describe the texture. This treat on a stick is made from sticky rice cooked in pork blood. Once firm, the warm cake is usually dipped in a soy-pork broth or sweet and sour sauce and rolled in cilantro and sweet peanut powder. The origins of such a dish likely date back to old days when farmers did not want to waste the blood that drained from ducks that they had slaughtered. Duck meat and blood are valuable in Chinese medicine, so making a rice cake from the duck blood was not only frugal, but also healthy. Visitors to Taichung City can enjoy the best pig's blood rice cake in Fengjia Night Market in Taichung County. This night market is the second largest in Taiwan.

　　串在竹籤上的豬血糕在很多台灣夜市都有賣。這個名字也許太真實了一點，但它的成分和質感對於吃香腸的人來說並不是完全陌生，特別是歐洲傳統的香腸，如來自法國的 boudin。口感紮實也有嚼勁是很多人描述吃豬血糕的感覺。豬血糕由糯米加豬血所煮成的。一旦蒸熟成型後，熱熱的豬血糕通常沾醬吃或裹上香菜和花生粉。這個小吃的起源可能要追溯到以前農民不想浪費他們宰殺的鴨子所排出的血液。鴨肉和血在中藥裡是很有價值的，所以用鴨血所做的豬血糕不僅節儉，而且還健康。隨著時間的轉換，與豬肉比起來鴨肉變得更加昂貴，所以豬血就取代鴨血來做豬血糕。遊客可以在台中的逢甲夜市吃到最好的豬血糕。逢甲夜市是台灣第二大夜市。

此部分為**聽、讀雙效「填空」練習**，現在就一起動身，開始聽「短段落」，提升常考字彙、語感等答題能力！

Pig's blood rice cake is served on a 1.＿＿＿＿＿＿＿ in many night markets in Taiwan. The name is perhaps a little too 2.＿＿＿＿＿＿＿ for some, but the ingredients and 3.＿＿＿＿＿＿＿ are not completely 4.＿＿＿＿＿＿＿ to anyone who eats 5.＿＿＿＿＿＿＿, especially traditional European forms like boudin from 6.＿＿＿＿＿＿＿. Firm, yet chewy is the best way to 7.＿＿＿＿＿＿＿ the texture. This treat on a stick is made from sticky rice cooked in pork blood. Once firm, the warm cake is usually 8.＿＿＿＿＿＿＿ in a soy-pork broth or sweet and sour sauce and rolled in cilantro and sweet peanut 9.＿＿＿＿＿＿＿. The 10.＿＿＿＿＿＿＿ of such a dish likely date back to old 11.＿＿＿＿＿＿＿ when 12.＿＿＿＿＿＿＿ did not want to waste the 13.＿＿＿＿＿＿＿ that drained from ducks that they had 14.＿＿＿＿＿＿＿. Duck meat and blood are 15.＿＿＿＿＿＿＿ in Chinese medicine, so making a rice cake from the duck blood was not only 16.＿＿＿＿＿＿＿, but also 17.＿＿＿＿＿＿＿. Visitors to Taichung City can enjoy the best pig's blood rice cake in Feng-jia Night Market in Taichung County. This night market is the 18.＿＿＿＿＿＿＿ largest in Taiwan.

▶▶ 參考答案

1. stick	2. honest
3. texture	4. unfamiliar
5. sausage	6. France
7. describe	8. dipped
9. powder	10. origins
11. days	12. farmers
13. blood	14. slaughtered
15. valuable	16. frugal
17. healthy	18. second

❶ Pig's blood rice cake is served on a _____ in many night markets in Taiwan.

❷ ingredients and texture: familiar with _____

❸ boudin: a dish from _____

❹ Pig's blood rice: sticky rice cooked in pork _____

❺ Pig's blood rice: rolled in cilantro and sweet peanut _____

_____

❻ origin: fluids from _____

❼ value: duck meat and blood possess _____ properties

❽ advantages: healthy and _____

Part 1 生活類主題

Part 2 學術類主題

❶ stick

❷ sausage

❸ France

❹ blood

❺ powder

❻ duck

❼ medicinal

❽ frugal

新竹－紅豆餅

Hsinchu city Imagawayaki

▶▶ 影子跟讀「短段落」練習 🎧 MP3 014

　　此篇為「**影子跟讀短段落練習**」，規劃了由聽「**短段落**」的 shadowing 練習，強化聽力專注力和掌握各個考點！

　　Japanese's rule over Taiwan from 1895 to 1945 influenced the island's appearance as well as its cuisine. Japan sought to make Taiwan a model colony and produced an economy that would further aid its expansionist plans. So, Japan poured many resources into the island, modernizing roads, rail, energy, and helping to boost Taiwan into the industrial powerhouse it is today. Imagawayaki (red bean pastry) is a traditional dessert dating from Japan's 18th century that is still a welcome by-product of Japan's colonization of Taiwan. It is essentially a pancake batter, cooked in a special griddle that looks like a giant western muffin tin or open waffle iron with round holes instead of square holes. As the batter begins to cook, the vendor adds a large spoonful of filling on top of the batter. The most traditional type is red bean paste, though more street market stalls are also selling custard, peanut, Asian cabbage, dried turnip, and curry-filled imagawayaki. "Zhu Cheng Red Bean Pastry" is a famous place for red bean pastry in northern Hsinchu City. They sell red bean pastry with a variety of fillings such as red bean, cream butter, taro paste, sesame, dried radish and cabbage.

　　日本從 1895 年到 1945 年 統治台灣也同時影響了台灣的飲食。日本有心要把台灣建立為一個模範 殖民地以進一步的邁向日本擴張領土的目的。所以日本在台灣這個島嶼上投入了很多的資源，改建道路、鐵路、能源設施，這些後來都是幫助台灣走向工業轉型的重要背景。「紅豆餅」也就是車輪餅是一個傳統的甜點，其歷史可以追溯到日本的 18 世紀，這個小吃現在在台灣仍然很受歡迎。基本上是把麵糊倒入特殊的鐵鑄模烘烤，模子看起來像一個巨大的西式鬆餅烤具或是開放式有鐵圓孔的鬆餅，而不是一般的方型孔。麵糊煎熟後中央再填入餡，再取兩片餅皮夾合就完成。竹城紅豆餅在新竹市很受歡迎，賣的內餡有奶油，花生，最近幾年還有鹹味的紅豆餅，內餡高麗菜，蘿蔔乾甚至有咖哩內餡。賣的口味有：紅豆、奶油、芋頭、芝麻、菜脯和高麗菜。

此部分為**聽、讀雙效「填空」練習**，現在就一起動身，開始聽「短段落」，提升常考字彙、語感等答題能力！

Japanese's rule over Taiwan from 1._____ to 2._____ _____ influenced the island's 3._____ as well as its cuisine. Japan sought to make Taiwan a model 4._____ and produced an 5._____ that would further aid its expansionist 6._____. So, Japan poured many 7._____ _____ into the island, modernizing 8._____, rail, energy, and helping to boost Taiwan into the 9._____ powerhouse it is today. Imagawayaki (red bean pastry) is a traditional dessert dating from Japan's 18th 10._____ that is still a welcome by-product of Japan's 11._____ of Taiwan. It is 12._____ a pancake batter, cooked in a special griddle that looks like a giant western muffin tin or open waffle iron with round holes instead of 13._____ holes. As the batter begins to cook, the vendor adds a large spoonful of filling on top of the batter. The most 14._____ type is 15._____ _____ bean paste, though more street market stalls are also selling custard, peanut, Asian 16._____, dried turnip, and curry-filled imagawayaki. "Zhu Cheng Red Bean Pastry" is a famous place for red bean pastry in 17._____ Hsinchu City. They sell red bean pastry with a variety of fillings such as red bean, cream butter, taro paste, 18._____, dried radish and cabbage.

▶▶ 參考答案

1. 1895
2. 1945
3. appearance
4. colony
5. economy
6. plans
7. resources
8. roads
9. industrial
10. century
11. colonization
12. essentially
13. square
14. traditional
15. red
16. cabbage
17. northern
18. sesame

❶ Japanese's ruling: 1895 to _____

❷ expansionist plans: make Taiwan a model _____

❸ industrial powerhouse: modernizing roads, rail, _____
   __

❹ red bean pastry: can be traced back to _____ century

❺ making: in a special _____

❻ holes: _____ holes rather square holes

❼ on top of the batter: _____ will be added

❽ other flavors: red bean, cream butter, taro paste, sesame, dried radish and _____.

❶ 1945

❷ colony

❸ energy

❹ 18th

❺ griddle

❻ round

❼ filling

❽ cabbage

桃園－刨冰山
Taoyuan Shaved Ice Mountain

▶▶ 影子跟讀「短段落」練習 🎧 MP3 015

此篇為「**影子跟讀短段落練習**」，規劃了由聽「**短段落**」的 shadowing 練習，強化聽力專注力和掌握各個考點！

Bao Bing is "a dessert made of shaved or finely crushed ice with flavoring." It is called Tsu Bing in Taiwanese. It makes sense to call it "Shaved Ice" in English. In general, shaved ice mountain consists of a big pile of tiny ice pieces, topped with sweet fruit like mango and sweetened condensed milk. The ice itself is incredibly fine and more similar to snow than crushed ice. A more traditional version is smaller and includes tapioca balls. It's quite easy to find shaved ice mountain with every variety of fruit imaginable, sweetened red beans, taro root, sweet potato and tapioca pearls. Another common and unique topping for shaved ice mountain is aiyu jelly. Aiyu jelly is made from a type of fig found in Taiwan, although the jelly has little flavor of its own. It just adds a wiggly, squishy texture to the popular dessert. Another very unique and traditional shaved ice is banana ice. There were no fancy toppings in the olden days when resources were very limited. Banana ice is just water mixed with sugar and banana flavoring. Freeze the mixture to form a big square ice then shave it finely. That is the old time favorite banana ice.

　　刨冰就是一種「削薄的冰上面加調味的甜點」，台語又稱為剉冰。用英文「Shaved Ice」來翻譯這個美食是很有道理的。一般的刨冰就是將冰切細後在冰的上面加上水果如芒果和煉乳。刨冰的冰是刨得很綿細，比冰塊還像雪片。有些更傳統的冰更是在綿細冰上面加上粉圓。刨冰的配料有各種水果、紅豆、芋頭、甜番薯、粉圓和珍珠都可以加。另一種常見和獨特的配料是愛玉凍。愛玉果凍是由一種在台灣生長的一種無花果所製成的，這種果凍有很特殊的味道。加了愛玉的冰吃起來有軟軟的口感很受歡迎。香蕉冰是另一種很傳統也很特別的味道。以前物資缺少的年代是加上這麼多料的冰，通常是用最便宜的用料作出最好吃的風味，於是在清冰裡加了食用性香蕉水拌入白砂糖，結凍後，即可刨成可口的香蕉冰。

此部分為**聽、讀雙效「填空」練習**，現在就一起動身，開始聽「短段落」，提升常考字彙、語感等答題能力！

Bao Bing is "a dessert made of shaved or 1._____ crushed ice with flavoring." It is called Tsu Bing in Taiwanese. It makes sense to call it "Shaved Ice" in English. In general, shaved ice mountain consists of a 2._____ pile of tiny ice pieces, topped with 3._____ fruit like mango and sweetened 4._____ milk. The ice itself is incredibly fine and more similar to 5._____ than crushed ice. A more traditional version is smaller and includes tapioca balls. It's quite easy to find shaved ice mountain with every variety of fruit 6._____, sweetened red beans, taro 7._____, sweet potato and tapioca pearls. Another common and unique topping for shaved ice mountain is aiyu jelly. Aiyu jelly is made from a type of 8._____ found in Taiwan, although the jelly has little 9._____ of its own. It just adds a wiggly, squishy texture to the popular 10._____. Another very unique and traditional shaved ice is 11._____ ice. There were no 12._____ toppings in the olden days when 13._____ were very limited. Banana ice is just 14._____ mixed with sugar and banana flavoring. 15._____ the mixture to form a big square ice then shave it finely. That is the 16._____ time favorite banana ice.

▶▶ 參考答案

1. finely	2. big
3. sweet	4. condensed
5. snow	6. imaginable
7. root	8. fig
9. flavor	10. dessert
11. banana	12. fancy
13. resources	14. water
15. Freeze	16. old

Part 1 生活類主題

Part 2 學術類主題

❶ Shaved Ice: the translation of Bao Bing in _____

❷ fruit/topping: _____

❸ condiment/topping: sweetened condensed _____

❹ analogy: the same as _____

❺ other toppings: red beans, taro root, sweet _____ and tapioca _____.

❻ making of the jelly: a type of _____

❼ banana ice: without _____ toppings

❽ banana ice: just _____ mixed with sugar and banana flavoring

❶ English

❷ mango

❸ milk

❹ snow

❺ potato, pearls

❻ fig

❼ fancy

❽ water

台北－鐵蛋

Taipei Iron Egg

▶▶ 影子跟讀「短段落」練習 🎧 MP3 016

　　此篇為「**影子跟讀短段落練習**」，規劃了由聽「**短段落**」的 shadowing 練習，強化聽力專注力和掌握各個考點！

　　Iron egg, fried fish cracker, and A-Gei (stuffed tofu) are delicious delicacies native to the northern fishing village of Danshui. The origins behind these foods tell stories of fish villagers' frugal way of life regarding not wasting any food. Iron egg is a way to preserve the eggs by re-cooking and re-serving leftover eggs. Fried fish cracker is also a way to preserve abundant fish caught in the river of Danshui at a time when there was no refrigeration system. The story behind A-Gei is a cook's reinvention from leftover scrap food. Iron eggs are made by simmering hard-boiled eggs in soy sauce and spices, then drying and repeating the process for several days. Because of the long cooking time, iron eggs are black or brownish-black and their texture is rubbery and tough. The locals love the chewy experience of enjoying an iron egg. Quail eggs are the traditional type of egg used to make iron eggs, so the resulting snack is much smaller than a conventional chicken egg. Danshui was not always the laid-back tourist-friendly town on the northern edge of Taipei, but once a focal point of Spanish settlement in the 1600s and then a key to Japan's colony on Taiwan during the first half of the 1900s.

　　鐵蛋、魚酥、阿給這些美味佳餚都是原產於淡水北部的漁村。這些美食故事的背後都在訴說著早期漁村生活不想浪費任何食物的哲學。鐵蛋是一種以再煮過,或儲備剩蛋的方式來保存蛋,魚酥也是在彼時沒有冰箱的年代,為了保存從淡水河中所捕獲的漁獲而衍生的。阿給的由來是為了不想浪費賣剩下的食材所研發的獨特小吃。鐵蛋的作法是用醬油及五香配方的滷料煮過後,再風乾,此道程序要重覆幾天才算完成。因為長時間的滷煮,鐵蛋呈黑或黑褐色,口感有彈性且硬。當地人喜歡鐵蛋的嚼勁。傳統的鐵蛋是用鵪鶉蛋,這樣做出來的鐵蛋會比一般的雞蛋小很多。早期的淡水並非像現在給人的印象是台北北部的悠閒觀光小鎮,17 世紀時西班牙曾把這裡當殖民地,在 20 世紀上半葉時,日本人把這裡當成殖民台灣的一個關鍵的地方。

此部分為**聽、讀雙效「填空」練習**，現在就一起動身，開始聽「短段落」，提升常考字彙、語感等答題能力！

Iron egg, fried fish cracker, and A-Gei (stuffed tofu) are 1._____ _____ delicacies 2._____ to the northern fishing 3._____ of Danshui. The 4._____ behind these foods tell 5._____ of fish villagers' 6._____ way of life regarding not 7._____ any food. Iron egg is a way to 8._____ the eggs by re-cooking and re-serving leftover eggs. Fried fish cracker is also a way to preserve 9._____ _____ fish caught in the 10._____ of Danshui at a time when there was no 11._____ system. The story behind A-Gei is a cook's 12._____ from leftover scrap food. Iron eggs are made by simmering hard-boiled eggs in soy sauce and 13._____, then drying and repeating the 14._____ for several days. Because of the long cooking time, iron eggs are black or brownish-black and their texture is 15._____ and 16._____. The locals love the chewy experience of enjoying an iron egg. Quail eggs are the traditional type of egg used to make iron eggs, so the resulting 17._____ _____ is much smaller than a conventional chicken egg. Danshui was not always the laid-back 18._____ town on the northern edge of Taipei, but once a focal point of 19._____ _____ settlement in the 1600s and then a key to Japan's colony on Taiwan during the first half of the 20._____.

▶▶ 參考答案

1. delicious	2. native
3. village	4. origins
5. stories	6. frugal
7. wasting	8. preserve
9. abundant	10. river
11. refrigeration	12. reinvention
13. spices	14. process
15. rubbery	16. tough
17. snack	18. tourist-friendly
19. Spanish	20. 1900s

❶ origin: indigenous to the northern fishing _____ of Danshui

❷ villagers' way of life: _____

❸ Iron egg: use _____ eggs

❹ Fried fish cracker: created when no _____ system was invented.

❺ Iron eggs: simmering hard-boiled eggs in _____ and spices

❻ traditional iron eggs: use _____ eggs that is much smaller

❼ early Danshui: was colonized by _____ in the 1600s

❽ early Danshui: a _____ of Japan

❶ village

❷ frugal

❸ leftover

❹ refrigeration

❺ soy sauce

❻ quail

❼ Spain

❽ colony

屏東－胡椒蝦
Pingtung Pepper Shrimp

▶▶ 影子跟讀「短獨白」練習 🎧 MP3 017

此篇為**「影子跟讀短獨白練習」**，規劃了由聽**「短獨白」**的 shadowing 練習，強化聽力專注力和掌握各個考點，現在就一起動身，開始聽「短獨白」！

In many tropical, coastal areas of the world, shrimp is a staple food. Cultivating shrimp in small agricultural settings goes back to at least the 15th century in southeast Asia. Taiwan was an early adopter of fish farming on an industrial scale in the southern part of the island and quickly became one of the largest suppliers of exported shrimp. Sadly, the industry and the environment suffered great losses due to unsustainable practices during the 1980s. Since shrimp are relatively easy to grow and need only six months to mature from an egg to an adult shrimp, it's not surprising that shrimp is an ingredient in many traditional dishes in Taiwan. Taiwanese believe that shrimp are the sweetest when cooked in the shell. Among the dishes you may encounter in Taiwan are shrimp ball soup, shrimp in braised cabbage or stir-fried noodles, and pepper shrimp. Pepper shrimp is a relatively simple dish, made by soaking the whole unpeeled shrimp in rice wine, lightly breading it to deep fry it and then tossing in a pan for a quick stir fry with oil, garlic, ginger, and other spices. The shrimp is then beautifully arranged on a plate to be shared.

　　在世界許多熱帶沿海地區，蝦是一種主食。在東南亞小型的蝦養殖可以追溯到至少 15 世紀。台灣是最早在南部以產業規模做蝦養殖，並迅速成為出口蝦的最大供應商之一。不幸的是，在 80 年代期間的產業和環境，因為不當做法而遭受巨大損失。由於蝦是相對容易生長，由蝦卵到成蝦的成熟只需要六個月的成長期，所以在台灣許多傳統菜餚把蝦當作食材並不奇怪。台灣人認為，帶殼煮蝦最能煮出蝦的甜味。在台灣會常看到的蝦料理有蝦丸湯、麻油蝦、炒麵加蝦和胡椒蝦。胡椒蝦是很簡單的一道菜，把未去皮的蝦浸泡在米酒裡，輕輕裹上麵包屑後炸到金黃，撈起後在鍋裡加油和大蒜、生薑等香料快速翻炒就是一道簡單的胡椒蝦。出菜時，胡椒蝦漂亮地被鋪排在盤子上。

▶▶ 聽、讀雙效「填空」練習 🎧 MP3 017

此部分為**聽、讀雙效「填空」練習**，現在就一起動身，開始聽「短段落」，提升常考字彙、語感等答題能力！

In many tropical, 1._____ areas of the world, shrimp is a 2._____ food. Cultivating shrimp in small 3._____ settings goes back to at least the 15th century in 4._____ Asia. Taiwan was an early 5._____ of fish farming on an 6._____ scale in the southern part of the island and quickly became one of the largest 7._____ of exported shrimp. Sadly, the industry and the 8._____ suffered great losses due to 9._____ practices during the 1980s. Since shrimp are 10._____ easy to grow and need only six 11._____ to mature from an egg to an adult shrimp, it's not surprising that shrimp is an 12._____ in many traditional dishes in Taiwan. Taiwanese believe that shrimp are the 13._____ when cooked in the 14._____. Among the dishes you may encounter in Taiwan are shrimp ball soup, shrimp in braised 15._____ or stir-fried 16._____, and pepper shrimp. Pepper shrimp is a relatively simple dish, made by soaking the whole 17._____ shrimp in rice wine, lightly breading it to 18._____ fry it and then tossing in a pan for a quick stir fry with oil, 19._____, ginger, and other spices. The shrimp is then beautifully arranged on a 20._____ to be shared.

▶▶ 參考答案

1. coastal	2. staple
3. agricultural	4. southeast
5. adopter	6. industrial
7. suppliers	8. environment
9. unsustainable	10. relatively
11. months	12. ingredient
13. sweetest	14. shell
15. cabbage	16. noodles
17. unpeeled	18. deep
19. garlic	20. plate

❶ timeframe/cultivating shrimp: _____ century

❷ Taiwan: one of the largest _____ of exported shrimp

❸ during the 1980s: _____ practices

❹ time for the shrimp to reach adulthood: only _____ months

❺ sweetest flavor: cooked in the _____

❻ one of the dishes: shrimp ball _____

❼ pepper shrimp: marinate in _____

❽ other way: a quick fry with oil in a _____

❶ 15th

❷ suppliers

❸ unsustainable

❹ six

❺ shell

❻ soup

❼ rice wine

❽ pan

桃園－餡餅

Taoyuan Chinese Meat Pie

▶▶ 影子跟讀「短段落」練習 🎧 MP3 018

　　此篇為**「影子跟讀短段落練習」**，規劃了由聽**「短段落」**的 shadowing 練習，強化聽力專注力和掌握各個考點！

　　Chinese meat pie is a simple, tasty snack of dough, filled with pork or beef and vegetables: onions or green onion, etc. Also in the meat mixture are traditional spices and flavors: soy sauce, ginger, garlic, eggs, sesame oil, pepper, salt, and sometimes monosodium glutamate. After the cook makes the simple wheat dough, he adds raw beef mixture, wraps dough around the beef and pan fries 3-4 minutes per side. The result is a lovely, compact, round packet that is crispy on the top and bottom, soft on the sides, and really juicy on the inside. Common Chinese meat pies you can buy in Taiwan are a round shape, about 10 cm in diameter. Many foods from China come with a myth about how the food originated. In the case of Chinese Meat Pie, there are stories about an emperor who disguised himself in order to sample the rustic, local fare. He thought the pies were so delicious, and so much better than what he was served at the palace. He even commemorated the flavor with a hastily scribed poem.

餡餅是一種很簡單好吃的小吃，基本上是麵團裡包入豬肉餡或牛肉餡，加入蔬菜洋蔥或蔥等。另外在肉裡也會加入傳統的調料和香料：醬油、薑、蒜頭、雞蛋、香油、鹽，有時也會加味精。麵團做好後就可包入肉餡，然後兩邊各煎 3-4 分鐘即可。這樣就做出了小巧、紮實，上下表皮都酥脆，內餡柔軟多汁的圓餡餅。台灣攤販所賣的餡餅通常是一個 10 公分大小的圓形。很多中國食品的起源都有點神話般。就餡餅來說，有一個皇帝把自己喬裝就為了要品嚐當地的美食。他覺得餡餅很好吃，而且比任何他在皇殿裡所端上來的食物好吃多了。他甚至還匆匆的自己寫下一首詩來回味這個味道。

　　此部分為**聽、讀雙效「填空」練習**，現在就一起動身，開始聽「短段落」，提升常考字彙、語感等答題能力！

　　Chinese meat pie is a simple, tasty snack of dough, filled with 1._____ or 2._____ and vegetables: onions or green onion, etc. Also in the meat mixture are traditional spices and flavors: soy sauce, ginger, garlic, eggs, sesame 3._____, pepper, salt, and sometimes monosodium glutamate. After the 4._____ makes the simple wheat dough, he adds raw beef mixture, wraps dough around the beef and pan fries 3-4 5._____ per side. The 6._____ is a lovely, compact, round packet that is 7._____ on the top and bottom, 8._____ on the sides, and really 9._____ on the inside. Common Chinese meat pies you can buy in Taiwan are a 10._____ shape, about 10 cm in 11._____. Many foods from China come with a 12._____ about how the food 13._____. In the case of Chinese Meat Pie, there are stories about an 14._____ who 15._____ himself in order to 16._____ the rustic, local fare. He thought the pies were so delicious, and so much better than what he was served at the 17._____. He even commemorated the flavor with a hastily scribed 18._____.

▶▶ 參考答案

1.	pork	2.	beef
3.	oil	4.	cook
5.	minutes	6.	result
7.	crispy	8.	soft
9.	juicy	10.	round
11.	diameter	12.	myth
13.	originated	14.	emperor
15.	disguised	16.	sample
17.	palace	18.	poem

❶ Chinese meat pie: full of _____ and vegetables.

❷ ingredients: include monosodium _____

❸ procedure: the cook adds _____ that is raw

❹ taste: _____ on the top and bottom; _____ on the inside

❺ shape of common Chinese meat pies: _____

❻ shape of common Chinese meat pies: _____ cm in diameter

❼ story: an _____ got concealed to sample the dish

❽ recollection: by writing a _____

Part 1 生活類主題

Part 2 學術類主題

❶ meat

❷ glutamate

❸ beef

❹ crispy, juicy

❺ round

❻ 10

❼ emperor

❽ poem

南投－傳統口味營養三明治
Nantou-Taiwanese Old Style Sandwich

▶▶ 影子跟讀「短段落」練習 🎧 MP3 019

　　此篇為**「影子跟讀短段落練習」**，規劃了由聽**「短段落」**的 shadowing 練習，強化聽力專注力和掌握各個考點！

　　Taiwanese old style or nutritious sandwich uses a warm and crispy deep fried doughnut-type bread, sliced and filled with tomatoes and cucumbers, ham or sausage, slices of braised hard-boiled egg and Taiwanese sweet mayonnaise. The origins of this sandwich are unknown, and even the mayonnaise may seem out of place from a western point of view. In fact, mayonnaise is the second most popular condiment in nearby Japan – second only to the ubiquitous soy sauce. Mayonnaise was probably introduced to East Asia from Europe some time during the 19th century. Now, mayonnaise has grown to such a high position in Japan that there is a mayonnaise museum called Mayo Terrace. Mayonnaise is so popular in Taiwan and Japan that American restaurant chains like Pizza Hut put mayonnaise on top of pizza in those countries. While this may sound bizarre to western tastes, globalization of food is not a new thing. Even in the 13th century, Marco Polo, the famous Italian explorer, is part of a legend in which he carries noodles from China back home to Italy. However, Italy strongly protests against the idea that China invented noodles and notes that there is no archeological evidence to support the idea.

　　台灣古早味營養三明治是用炸過類似甜甜圈麵團的麵包，切片後加了番茄和黃瓜、火腿或香腸、滷蛋以及台式甜味美奶滋。這種三明治的起源無可考，西方人更想不到會有台式美奶滋這種醬料。事實上，美奶滋在日本是第二個最流行的調味品，僅次於無處不有的醬油。美奶滋可能在 19 世紀由歐洲傳入東亞。現在，美奶滋已經在日本有很崇高的地位，甚至有美乃滋展示館。美乃滋在台灣和日本非常受歡迎，美國的連鎖餐廳像必勝客會把美乃滋加在比薩餅上面。這對西方人來說聽起來匪夷所思，但食物的全球化不是最近才有的。甚至在 13 世紀，有關義大利著名的探險家馬可波羅有一個傳說，他把來自中國的麵條帶回老家義大利。然而，義大利對於中國發明麵條的說法是強烈抗議，表明沒有考古證據。

此部分為**聽、讀雙效「填空」練習**，現在就一起動身，開始聽「短段落」，提升常考字彙、語感等答題能力！

Taiwanese old style or 1._____ sandwich uses a warm and crispy deep fried doughnut-type bread, sliced and filled with 2._____ and 3._____, ham or sausage, slices of braised hardboiled egg and Taiwanese sweet 4._____. The 5._____ of this sandwich are 6._____, and even the mayonnaise may seem out of place from a western point of view. In fact, mayonnaise is the second most popular 7._____ in nearby Japan – second only to the 8._____ soy sauce. Mayonnaise was probably 9._____ to East Asia from 10._____ some time during the 19th century. Now, mayonnaise has grown to such a high position in Japan that there is a mayonnaise museum called Mayo Terrace. Mayonnaise is so 11._____ in Taiwan and Japan that American 12._____ chains like Pizza Hut put mayonnaise on top of pizza in those 13._____. While this may sound 14._____ to western tastes, 15._____ of food is not a new thing. Even in the 13th century, Marco Polo, the famous 16._____ explorer, is part of a 17._____ in which he carries noodles from China back home to 18._____. However, Italy strongly protests against the idea that China invented noodles and notes that there is no 19._____ evidence to support the 20._____.

▶▶ 參考答案

1. nutritious	2. tomatoes
3. cucumbers	4. mayonnaise
5. origins	6. unknown
7. condiment	8. ubiquitous
9. introduced	10. Europe
11. popular	12. restaurant
13. countries	14. bizarre
15. globalization	16. Italian
17. legend	18. Italy
19. archeological	20. idea

❶ nutritious sandwich: use fruits and vegetables, such as _____ _____ and _____ will be added.

❷ origins of the sandwich: _____

❸ second most popular condiment: _____

❹ origins of mayonnaise: _____

❺ Mayo Terrace: a mayonnaise _____

❻ Pizza Hut: use mayonnaise on top of _____

❼ Marco Polo: the famous Italian _____

❽ Marco Polo: brings noodles back to his own country, _____ _____

❶ tomatoes, cucumbers

❷ unknown

❸ mayonnaise

❹ Europe

❺ museum

❻ pizza

❼ explorer

❽ Italy

南投－意麵
Nantou Noodles (Yi Mian)

▶▶ 影子跟讀「短段落」練習 🎧 MP3 020

　　此篇為「**影子跟讀短段落練習**」，規劃了由聽「**短段落**」的 shadowing 練習，強化聽力專注力和掌握各個考點！

　　Nantou, Taiwan's only landlocked county is famous for its yi mian. Some noodle makers sun dry yi mian in a big, flat bamboo basket. Dry yi mian can be kept longer. They look similar to what western consumers know as Ramen noodles. The noodle dough is unique because it traditionally includes duck egg whites and soda water. Ducks were a main staple food in agricultural Taiwan. Duck yolks are soaked in salt for different dishes, leaving the whites as unneeded leftovers. Adding duck egg whites to yi mian could just be a way to use all the leftover duck egg whites. The soda water helps the noodles retain their spongy texture. Nantou County in Taiwan is 83% mountainous with 41 peaks reaching over 3,000 meters (9,800 feet) high. Beautiful inland lakes and ponds, like Sun Moon Lake, are popular tourist destinations. Nantou is also home to a 1500+ acre amusement park and cultural history living museum called Formosan Aboriginal Culture Village. The park celebrates eleven aboriginal tribes by recreating their villages and staging traditional performances for park attendees. Among the tribes featured is the smallest of Taiwan's recognized tribes, the Thao, who still make their home around Sun Moon Lake in Nantou.

南投，台灣唯一處於內陸的地方，以意麵最有名。這細扁的麵條通常都加在麵湯中。有些意麵也會在大竹籠上日曬至乾燥以利保存。乾意麵可以保存更久，意麵看起來很類似西方消費者所知道的速食麵。意麵的麵團跟一般做麵的麵團來説是比較獨特，因為意麵的麵團用的是鴨蛋蛋白和蘇打水。鴨子在以前的農業台灣算是主食。鴨蛋黃被醃製後用在不同的料理，剩下的鴨蛋白很可能是因此廢物利用拿來做意麵。蘇打水有助於麵條保留其 QQ 的口感。南投縣內有台灣 83% 的山地，有 41 個山峰達到 3000 多公尺（9800 英尺）。這裡有美麗的內陸湖泊和池塘，像日月潭就是熱門的旅遊地。南投也有一個有 1500 英畝大的九族文化村，這是結合遊樂園和文化歷史生活館的觀光地。透過重建他們的村莊和傳統表演，九族文化村裡保留有 11 個原住民的傳統。其中很有特色的部落邵族是台灣官方承認最小的部落，他們的世代祖先都住在南投日月潭。

　　此部分為**聽、讀雙效「填空」練習**，現在就一起動身，開始聽「短段落」，提升常考字彙、語感等答題能力！

　　Nantou, Taiwan's only 1.＿＿＿＿＿＿＿ county is famous for its yi mian. Some noodle makers sun dry yi mian in a big, flat bamboo 2.＿＿＿＿＿＿＿. Dry yi mian can be kept longer. They look similar to what western 3.＿＿＿＿＿＿＿ know as Ramen noodles. The noodle dough is unique because it traditionally includes duck egg whites and 4.＿＿＿＿＿＿＿ water. Ducks were a main staple food in agricultural Taiwan. Duck 5.＿＿＿＿＿＿＿ are soaked in salt for different dishes, leaving the whites as 6.＿＿＿＿＿＿＿ leftovers. Adding duck egg whites to yi mian could just be a way to use all the leftover duck egg whites. The soda water helps the noodles 7.＿＿＿＿＿＿＿ their 8.＿＿＿＿＿＿＿ texture. Nantou County in Taiwan is 83% 9.＿＿＿＿＿＿＿ with 41 peaks reaching over 10.＿＿＿＿＿＿＿ meters (9,800 feet) high. Beautiful inland 11.＿＿＿＿＿＿＿ and 12.＿＿＿＿＿＿＿, like Sun Moon Lake, are popular tourist 13.＿＿＿＿＿＿＿. Nantou is also home to a 1500+ acre 14.＿＿＿＿＿＿＿ park and cultural history living 15.＿＿＿＿＿＿＿ called Formosan Aboriginal Culture Village. The park 16.＿＿＿＿＿＿＿ eleven aboriginal tribes by recreating their 17.＿＿＿＿＿＿＿ and staging traditional 18.＿＿＿＿＿＿＿ for park attendees. Among the tribes 19.＿＿＿＿＿＿＿ is the smallest of Taiwan's 20.＿＿＿＿＿＿＿ tribes, the Thao, who still make their home around Sun Moon

Lake in Nantou.

▶▶ 參考答案

1. landlocked	2. basket
3. consumers	4. soda
5. yolks	6. unneeded
7. retain	8. spongy
9. mountainous	10. 3,000
11. lakes	12. ponds
13. destinations	14. amusement
15. museum	16. celebrates
17. villages	18. performances
19. featured	20. recognized

❶ Nantou: is entirely surrounded by land, so it's _____

❷ yi mian: should be exposed to _____ in a basket

❸ noodle dough: includes duck egg whites and _____

❹ duck whites: as unnecessary _____

❺ texture: can be maintained _____ by using soda water

❻ Nantou County: _____ peaks

❼ representative of the tourist site: _____

❽ The park: retains _____ aboriginal tribes

❶ landlocked

❷ sun

❸ soda water

❹ leftovers

❺ spongy

❻ 41

❼ Sun Moon Lake

❽ eleven

UNIT 21

金門貢糖和高粱酒

Kinmen Peanut Candy and Kaoliang Liquor

▶▶ 影子跟讀「短段落」練習 🎧 MP3 021

此篇為「影子跟讀短段落練習」，規劃了由聽「短段落」的 shadowing 練習，強化聽力專注力和掌握各個考點！

Kinmen is a popular tourist destination that is known for quaint architecture and beaches. There are two specialty items a tourist should look for. The first is Kimen Peanut Candy. Many stores sell the peanut candy and most will encourage the buyer to try it before buying. However, buying the candy from a store that weighs it will give you more candy for the same price as the pre-boxed kind.

金門是一個有名的觀光景點，以古色古香的建築及其美麗的海灘而著稱。這裡有兩個旅客必看的項目。第一是金門貢糖。在金門街上有很多賣貢糖的店，很多店家也都會有試吃再買的服務，秤斤的貢糖會比較划算，秤斤與盒裝數量會差到至少二倍。

The second item is Kinmen Kaoliang Liquor which has a rich fragrance and is strong tasting. When compared to popular Taiwan alcohol, such as rice wine, wine, beer, and Shaoxing wine, the Kinmen Kaoliang Liquor has a higher alcohol concentration. Liquor in White Urn (with a 58.38 % alcoholic concentration) can only be bought in Kinmen. Warning: there are still mines in Kinmen. Although the mined area has signs, tourists still need to be careful and not mistakenly step on one!

　　再來是金門的高粱酒，因為氣候的關係以高粱釀出的酒醞育出芬芳氣味和濃郁口味，對於酒外行的遊客來説，到金門買高粱酒要注意的是，比起一般在臺灣普遍的米酒，葡萄酒，啤酒和紹興酒來説，酒精濃度高很多，像是只能在金門買到的白色甕裝，含有濃度 58%的酒精。金門的太陽很強烈，出門一定要注意防曬，另外要注意的就是金門現在還是有很多的地雷，雖然地雷區都會有標示，但是還是小心不要誤踩！

　　此部分為**聽、讀雙效「填空」練習**，現在就一起動身，開始聽「短段落」，提升常考字彙、語感等答題能力！

　　Kinmen is a popular 1.＿＿＿＿＿＿＿ destination that is known for 2.＿＿＿＿＿＿ architecture and 3.＿＿＿＿＿＿. There are 4.＿＿＿＿＿＿ specialty items a tourist should look for. The first is Kimen Peanut Candy. Many stores sell the peanut 5.＿＿＿＿＿＿ and most will 6.＿＿＿＿＿＿ the buyer to try it before buying. However, buying the candy from a 7.＿＿＿＿＿＿ that 8.＿＿＿＿＿＿ it will give you more candy for the same 9.＿＿＿＿ as the 10.＿＿＿＿＿＿ kind.

　　The second item is Kinmen Kaoliang 11.＿＿＿＿＿＿ which has a rich 12.＿＿＿＿＿＿ and is 13.＿＿＿＿＿＿ tasting. When compared to popular Taiwan alcohol, such as rice wine, wine, 14.＿＿＿＿＿＿, and Shaoxing wine, the Kinmen Kaoliang Liquor has a higher 15.＿＿＿＿＿＿ concentration. Liquor in White Urn (with a 58.38 % alcoholic concentration) can only be bought in Kinmen. Warning: there are still 16.＿＿＿＿＿＿ in Kinmen. Although the mined area has 17.＿＿＿＿＿＿, tourists still need to be careful and not 18.＿＿＿＿＿＿ step on one!

▶▶ 參考答案

1. tourist	2. quaint
3. beaches	4. two
5. candy	6. encourage
7. store	8. weighs
9. price	10. pre-boxed
11. Liquor	12. fragrance
13. strong	14. beer
15. alcohol	16. mines
17. signs	18. mistakenly

❶ Kinmen: a popular _____ destination

❷ first item: Kimen Peanut _____

❸ candy: the _____ contains less candy

❹ Kinmen Kaoliang Liquor: contains an abundant _____
___

❺ Kinmen Kaoliang Liquor: its flavor is _____

❻ Kinmen Kaoliang Liquor: _____ concentration higher than other brands

❼ White Urn kind/concentration: _____ %

❽ danger: there is still a chance for tourists to step on _____
_____

Part 1 生活類主題

Part 2 學術類主題

❶ tourist

❷ Candy

❸ pre-boxed

❹ fragrance

❺ strong

❻ alcohol

❼ 58.38

❽ mines

UNIT 22

臺灣烏龍茶

此篇為「**影子跟讀短段落練習**」，規劃了由聽「**短段落**」的 shadowing 練習，強化聽力專注力和掌握各個考點！

There are many different types of Taiwan oolong tea, such as Jin Xuan tea and Evergreen tea. Any tea that is fermented between 30 to 40 degrees Celsius can use the oolong tea label. Oolong's unique process is that after it's dried, the leaves are wrapped in a ball with a cloth and rolled back and forth until eventually the leaves are semi-fermented and hemispherical. Handpicked oolong tea leaves have one heart with three or two leaves. The final product is a hemispherical tea. After brewing, the tea is golden amber color and has a sweet taste.

臺灣烏龍茶的種類很多，例如金萱、松柏長青茶等，所有發酵三十至四十度之間做法的茶都可以被稱為烏龍茶。烏龍茶獨特的製茶過程是烘乾後再重複用布包成球狀揉捻茶葉，使茶葉呈半發酵、半球狀。手工摘取的烏龍茶有一心三葉或一心兩葉，成品的茶葉是半球狀，沖泡後，茶是金黃偏琥珀色，回甘十足。

One type of Taiwanese oolong tea is Dongding Oolong Tea which is also known as Dongding Tea. Dongding Mountain is located near Unicorn Lake in Lugu Township, Nantou County, Taiwan. Dongding Oolong Tea is famous in Taiwan, but most people don't know it's named after Dongding Mountain.

凍頂烏龍茶就是一種臺灣烏龍茶，又稱凍頂茶，「凍頂」是地名，就是位在臺灣南投縣鹿谷鄉「麒麟潭」邊的「凍頂山」，凍頂烏龍茶在臺灣很有名但是很多人都不知道這個茶名就是來自真名的「凍頂山」。

此部分為**聽、讀雙效「填空」練習**，現在就一起動身，開始聽「短段落」，提升常考字彙、語感等答題能力！

There are many different types of Taiwan oolong tea, such as Jin Xuan tea and 1._____ tea. Any tea that is 2._____ between 30 to 40 degrees 3._____ can use the oolong tea label. Oolong's 4._____ process is that after it's 5._____, the leaves are 6._____ in a ball with a 7._____ and rolled back and forth until eventually the 8._____ are semi-fermented and 9._____. 10._____ oolong tea leaves have one heart with three or two leaves. The final 11._____ is a hemispherical tea. After brewing, the tea is 12._____ amber 13._____ and has a sweet 14._____.

One 15._____ of Taiwanese oolong tea is Dongding Oolong Tea which is also known as Dongding Tea. Dongding Mountain is 16._____ near Unicorn Lake in Lugu Township, Nantou County, Taiwan. Dongding Oolong Tea is famous in Taiwan, but most people don't know it's named after Dongding Mountain.

▶▶ **參考答案**

1. Evergreen	2. fermented
3. Celsius	4. unique
5. dried	6. wrapped
7. cloth	8. leaves
9. hemispherical	10. Handpicked
11. product	12. golden
13. color	14. taste
15. type	16. located

❶ Taiwan oolong tea: Jin Xuan tea and _____ tea.

❷ oolong tea label: _____ between 30 to 40 degrees

❸ second procedure: the leaves are wrapped in a ball with a __ _____

❹ outcome: the leaves are semi-fermented and _____

❺ _____ oolong tea leaves: have one heart with three or two leaves

❻ color: _____ amber

❼ taste: _____

❽ location: near Unicorn _____

❶ Evergreen

❷ fermented

❸ cloth

❹ hemispherical

❺ Handpicked

❻ golden

❼ sweet

❽ Lake

高山茶
High Mountain Tea

▶▶ 影子跟讀「短段落」練習 🎧 MP3 023

此篇為**「影子跟讀短段落練習」**，規劃了由聽**「短段落」**的 shadowing 練習，強化聽力專注力和掌握各個考點！

"High Mountain Tea" does not refer to a specific place. Basically, all tea grown at an altitude of 100 meters above sea level can be called "High Mountain Tea". Many of Taiwan's existing mountain tea farms originally grew trees or bamboo. Over the years, these lands accumulated organic materials which provide good nutrients for tea plants.

「高山茶」其實是一般名詞，並不是指特定地方所製作的茶葉。基本上，生長於海拔 1,000 公尺以上茶園所製的茶葉就是高山茶。臺灣現有的高山茶園很多以前是林地竹地，土壤裡充足的養份來自常年累積的有機質堆積，成為種茶的好地方。

There are two advantages to growing tea in the high altitude. One is the cold climate and the short periods of daily sunshine, lowering the bitter components of tea and increasing the sweet taste. Second, due to temperature differences between day and night and the long afternoon clouds, tea grows slowly which results in softer shoots and thicker mesophyll.

高山種茶還需要有兩項優勢，一是高山氣候的冷涼和平均較短的日照，這樣可以讓茶樹芽葉的苦澀成分降低而提升甘味。二是日夜溫差大及午後雲霧遮蔽會讓茶樹的生長趨於緩慢，讓芽葉柔軟和葉肉厚實。

　　此部分為**聽、讀雙效「填空」練習**，現在就一起動身，開始聽「短段落」，提升常考字彙、語感等答題能力！

　　High Mountain Tea does not refer to a 1.＿＿＿＿＿＿ place. Basically, all tea grown at an 2.＿＿＿＿＿＿ of 100 meters above 3.＿＿＿＿＿＿ level can be called "High Mountain Tea". Many of Taiwan's 4.＿＿＿＿＿＿ mountain tea farms originally grew 5.＿＿＿＿＿＿ or 6.＿＿＿＿＿＿. Over the years, these lands 7.＿＿＿＿＿＿ organic 8.＿＿＿＿＿＿ which provide good 9.＿＿＿＿＿＿ for tea 10.＿＿＿＿＿＿.

　　There are two 11.＿＿＿＿＿＿ to growing tea in the 12.＿＿＿＿＿＿ altitude. One is the cold 13.＿＿＿＿＿＿ and the short periods of daily 14.＿＿＿＿＿＿, lowering the bitter 15.＿＿＿＿＿＿ of tea and increasing the sweet taste. Second, due to 16.＿＿＿＿＿＿ differences between day and night and the long afternoon 17.＿＿＿＿＿＿, tea grows slowly which results in 18.＿＿＿＿＿＿ shoots and thicker mesophyll.

▶▶ **參考答案**

1. specific	2. altitude
3. sea	4. existing
5. trees	6. bamboo
7. accumulated	8. materials
9. nutrients	10. plants
11. advantages	12. high
13. climate	14. sunshine
15. components	16. temperature
17. clouds	18. softer

❶ High Mountain Tea: at an altitude of _____ meters above sea level

❷ tea farms: originally grew trees or _____

❸ accumulation: _____ materials

❹ materials: provide good _____ for tea plants

❺ high altitude: cold _____ and the shorten _____
_____

❻ high altitude: fewer bitter _____

❼ high altitude: the _____ taste on the rise

❽ high altitude: slow _____ due to temperature fluctuations

❶ 100

❷ bamboo

❸ organic

❹ nutrients

❺ climate, sunshine

❻ components

❼ sweet

❽ growth

古坑咖啡
Gukeng Coffee

▶▶ 影子跟讀「短段落」練習 🎧 MP3 024

此篇為**「影子跟讀短段落練習」**，規劃了由聽「短段落」的 shadowing 練習，強化聽力專注力和掌握各個考點！

Locally grown coffee in Taiwan? Really? Yes! The home of Taiwanese coffee is in the Huashan area of Gukeng County in Yunlin, Taiwan. The Dutch brought coffee to Taiwan in 1924, but Japanese started growing coffee in Taiwan in 1941. They found the best place to grow coffee was in Gukeng County. After the war and the Japanese left Taiwan, the price for coffee beans wasn't competitive enough, so many coffee plantations were abandoned.

臺灣本土咖啡？真的嗎？真的。臺灣咖啡原產地是在臺灣雲林古坑縣的華山地區。臺灣最早的咖啡是由荷蘭人於 1924 年所引進，日本人在臺灣在 1941 年開始種植咖啡，他們發在古坑縣是種植咖啡的最佳場所。戰後日本人離開臺灣後，咖啡的價格沒有競爭性所以後來該地區大多數的咖啡種植園都荒廢了。

But in 2000, the Taiwanese government encouraged local growers to cultivate locally grown coffee again. The first Coffee Festival in Taiwan was held in Yunlin, in 2003, and "Gukeng Coffee" (a type of Arabica coffee) started gaining its reputation. After that, Taiwanese Coffee developed a market share. Although a lot of coffee is still imported in Taiwan, the locally grown coffee has the distinct taste due to different roasting, extraction method, and brewing time. Try a cup of Gukeng Coffee during your visit!

直到 2000 年，臺灣政府開始鼓勵當地人種植臺灣本地咖啡。在 2003 年，臺灣第一季咖啡節是在雲林舉行，「古坑咖啡」（阿拉比卡咖啡的種類）開始獲得聲譽。之後，臺灣咖啡開始在市場上佔有一席之地。雖然在臺灣有很多進口咖啡，當地種植的咖啡因為有不同的烘焙和萃取的方法所以具有特殊的味道。如果有機會的話，別忘了來一杯古坑咖啡！

此部分為**聽、讀雙效「填空」練習**，現在就一起動身，開始聽「短段落」，提升常考字彙、語感等答題能力！

Locally grown coffee in Taiwan? Really? Yes! The 1._____ _____ of Taiwanese coffee is in the Huashan area of Gukeng County in Yunlin, Taiwan. The 2._____ brought coffee to Taiwan in 3._____, but 4._____ started growing coffee in Taiwan in 5._____. They found the best place to grow coffee was in Gukeng County. After the 6._____ and the Japanese left Taiwan, the 7._____ for coffee beans wasn't 8._____ enough, so many coffee 9._____ were 10._____. But in 2000, the Taiwanese government encouraged local 11._____ to 12._____ locally grown coffee again. The first Coffee 13._____ in Taiwan was held in Yunlin, in 2003, and "Gukeng Coffee" (a type of Arabica coffee) started gaining its 14._____. After that, Taiwanese Coffee developed a 15._____ share. Although a lot of coffee is still imported in Taiwan, the locally grown coffee has the 16._____ taste due to different roasting, 17._____ method, and 18._____ time. Try a cup of Gukeng Coffee during your visit!

▶▶ 參考答案

1. home	2. Dutch
3. 1924	4. Japanese
5. 1941	6. war
7. price	8. competitive
9. plantations	10. abandoned
11. growers	12. cultivate
13. Festival	14. reputation
15. market	16. distinct
17. extraction	18. brewing

❶ introduction: by the _____

❷ introduction: in _____

❸ 1941: _____ started growing coffee

❹ the price for coffee beans: not _____

❺ coffee plantations: _____

❻ 2000: _____ locally grown coffee

❼ 2003: obtained _____

❽ distinct taste: due to different roasting, _____ method, and brewing time

❶ Dutch

❷ 1924

❸ Japanese

❹ competitive

❺ abandoned

❻ cultivate

❼ reputation

❽ extraction

庵古坑和橙之鄉
Um Gukeng and Orange County

▶▶ 影子跟讀「短段落」練習 🎧 MP3 025

此篇為**「影子跟讀短段落練習」**，規劃了由聽**「短段落」**的 shadowing 練習，強化聽力專注力和掌握各個考點！

In the past, Gukeng County was called Um Gukeng. Because of its climate and geology, Gukeng County is the main agricultural area in Taiwan. In recent years, this county became famous for its locally grown coffee, but many other agricultural crops grow here as well. The oranges grown here are the best in Taiwan and have given the county the nickname of Orange County. Beside oranges, other fruits grown here, such as grapefruit, mandarin oranges, and pineapple, are also outstanding. A lot of the fruit orchards encourage tourists to come and pick their own fruit right off the trees.

古坑鄉以前叫做「庵古坑」(Um Gukeng)，因為氣候和地質的關係，這裡是臺灣農業主要的產區，近年除了出產臺灣咖啡而大有名氣外，許多其他的農作物也耕種於此，這裡的柳丁產量也是全臺之冠，良好的柳丁品質讓這裡有了「橙之鄉」的美譽。除了柳丁之外，還有葡萄柚、柑桔、鳳梨都是很出色的當地出產水果，這裡有很多的觀光

果園可以讓遊客享受採收的樂趣。

Flowers from the citrus plants bloom from March to April in Um Gukeng, and a sea of white flowers from the citrus trees cover the whole town of Um Gukeng. When you are planning a trip to Um Gukeng, don't forget to include the annual blossom season.

「庵古坑」每年到了 3～4 月時就是柑橘類花朵盛開的時候，果樹上的花望眼看去好像鋪蓋了整個古坑，在做行程的設計時不要忘了考慮一年才開一次的橙花季節。

此部分為**聽、讀雙效「填空」練習**，現在就一起動身，開始聽「短段落」，提升常考字彙、語感等答題能力！

In the past, Gukeng County was called Um Gukeng. Because of its 1._____ and 2._____, Gukeng County is the main 3._____ area in Taiwan. In recent years, this county became 4._____ for its locally grown coffee, but many other agricultural 5._____ grow here as well. The 6._____ grown here are the best in Taiwan and have given the county the 7._____ of Orange County. Beside oranges, other fruits grown here, such as 8._____, mandarin oranges, and 9._____, are also 10._____. A lot of the fruit 11._____ encourage tourists to come and pick their own fruit right off the 12._____.

Flowers from the citrus plants bloom from 13._____ to 14._____ in Um Gukeng, and a sea of 15._____ flowers from the citrus trees cover the whole 16._____ of Um Gukeng. When you are planning a trip to Um Gukeng, don't forget to include the 17._____ 18._____ season.

▶▶ 參考答案

1. climate	2. geology
3. agricultural	4. famous
5. crops	6. oranges
7. nickname	8. grapefruit
9. pineapple	10. outstanding
11. orchards	12. trees
13. March	14. April
15. white	16. town
17. annual	18. blossom

Part 1 生活類主題

Part 2 學術類主題

❶ reason: climate and _____

❷ fame: due to its locally grown _____

❸ nickname: thanks to _____ grown here

❹ other fruits: _____ and _____

❺ Tourists will visit to the fruit _____

❻ Tourists are able to get the _____ from the trees.

❼ blossom: flowers from the _____ plants

❽ the color of the citrus flower: _____

❶ geology

❷ coffee

❸ oranges

❹ grapefruit, pineapple

❺ orchards

❻ fruit

❼ citrus

❽ white

惠蓀咖啡

Huisun Coffee

▶▶ 影子跟讀「短段落」練習 🎧 MP3 026

　　此篇為「影子跟讀短段落練習」，規劃了由聽「短段落」的 shadowing 練習，強化聽力專注力和掌握各個考點！

　　The Arabica coffee bean grown at the Huisun Farm was first introduced by the Japanese in 1936. The Huisin Farm has rich natural resources perfect for growing coffee but natural conditions, such as earthquakes, typhoons, and insect infestations destroy coffee plants and beans and affect the crops. A teaching and research farm, its main purpose is to promote local grown coffee as well as to assist farmers. Because the coffee from Huisun Farm is 100% locally grown, it tastes different from imported coffee due to the different climates and soils it's grown in. The end result is a neutral sweet taste full of aroma.

　　惠蓀林場的阿拉比卡咖啡豆最早是由日本人在 1936 引進種植。惠蓀林場的所在地的自然資源相當豐富，但是卻要克服種種的天然條件，如地震，風災，還有害蟲入侵會破壞咖啡樹和咖啡豆，進而影響農作物的生長。這是一個以學校生態植物教學研究為主，主要目的是提倡本土咖啡的種植和教育農夫，因為惠蓀林場的咖啡百分之百產自

於臺灣本土，也因氣候、水土等各方面不同，口味與進口之咖啡豆相比顯得中性、甘味、香氣十足。

In 2003, the official name for the coffee from Huisun was called "Taiwan Huisun Coffee" which is abbreviated to HS. This is a developing industry, and as farmers plant more coffee trees, set up more processing plants, refine the bean quality, and develop a market for locally grown coffee, it will expand.

在 2003 年正式以「臺灣惠蓀咖啡」行銷，惠蓀咖啡的縮寫是「HS」。這是一個發展中的行業，當農民種植更多的咖啡樹、設立了加工廠、精鍊咖啡豆的品質，並開發出當地種植咖啡的市場時，臺灣咖啡也將擴大佔領市場。

此部分為**聽、讀雙效「填空」練習**，現在就一起動身，開始聽「短段落」，提升常考字彙、語感等答題能力！

The Arabica coffee 1.＿＿＿＿＿＿ grown at the Huisun Farm was first 2.＿＿＿＿＿＿ by the Japanese in 3.＿＿＿＿ ＿＿. The Huisin Farm has rich 4.＿＿＿＿＿＿ resources perfect for growing coffee but natural conditions, such as 5.＿＿＿ ＿＿＿, 6.＿＿＿＿＿＿, and insect 7.＿＿＿＿＿＿ destroy coffee plants and beans and affect the crops. A teaching and 8.＿＿ ＿＿＿＿＿＿ farm, its main purpose is to 9.＿＿＿＿＿＿ local grown coffee as well as to 10.＿＿＿＿＿＿ farmers. Because the coffee from Huisun Farm is 100% locally grown, it tastes different from 11.＿＿＿＿＿＿ coffee due to the different climates and 12.＿＿＿＿＿＿ it's grown in. The end result is a 13.＿＿＿＿＿＿ sweet taste full of 14.＿＿＿＿＿＿. In 2003, the 15.＿＿＿＿＿＿ name for the coffee from Huisun was called "Taiwan Huisun Coffee" which is 16.＿＿＿＿＿＿ to HS. This is a 17.＿＿＿＿＿＿ industry, and as farmers plant more coffee trees, set up more 18.＿＿＿＿＿＿ plants, refine the bean 19.＿＿＿＿＿＿, and develop a market for locally grown coffee, it will 20.＿＿＿＿＿＿.

▶▶ 參考答案

1. bean	2. introduced
3. 1936	4. natural
5. earthquakes	6. typhoons
7. infestations	8. research
9. promote	10. assist
11. imported	12. soils
13. neutral	14. aroma
15. official	16. abbreviated
17. developing	18. processing
19. quality	20. expand

▶▶▶ **全真模擬試題練習** 🎧 MP3 026

❶ introduction: by Japanese in _____.

❷ The Huisin Farm: with bountiful natural _____

❸ natural phenomena: including insect _____ ruin coffee plants

❹ main purpose: provide _____ to farmers

❺ taste: due to various _____ and soils

❻ outcome: a neutral sweet taste filled with _____

❼ The _____ of Huisun Coffee is HS

❽ processing plants: make the bean _____ refined

❶ 1936

❷ resources

❸ infestations

❹ assistance

❺ climates

❻ aroma

❼ abbreviation

❽ quality

UNIT ㉗

北投溫泉
Bei Tou Hot Spring

▶▶ 影子跟讀「短段落」練習 🎧 MP3 027

此篇為 **「影子跟讀短段落練習」**，規劃了由聽 **「短段落」** 的 shadowing 練習，強化聽力專注力和掌握各個考點！

Imagine soaking at a naturally formed hot springs pool with steam rising from valley below in cold weather. Sounds like Heaven! In 1896, the Japanese built the first hot springs hotel in Taiwan called "Tengu Um house" in Bei Tou. They wanted to provide a place for the Japanese soldiers similar to the hot springs bath they had at home. It is still in business after all these years, but the name has changed to "Takimoto". A small monument stood in the front yard to commemorate the visit from the Crown Prince of Japan in 1923.

想想看，如果可以在冬天時，浸泡在自然形成的溫泉，而其蒸汽則是從下面的山谷所冒出，這聽起來是不是很像身在天堂！1896 年日本人在北投溫泉設立了臺灣第一家溫泉旅社叫「天狗庵旅舍」，就是目前還繼續經營的「瀧乃湯」。當時建立的目的主要是讓在臺灣的日本軍可以有泡湯的地方。在院子裡還可以看到「皇太子殿下御渡涉紀念碑」，這是紀念 1923 年日本皇太子裕仁來臺視察時有實際來到

北投。

　　Since it was built by Japanese, the architecture is quite unique when compared with the other large spa hotels in the area. In "Takimoto", there are separated baths for men and women. The naturally formed hot springs bath is very attractive to the visitors historically. Plus the low fee makes you want to return like the local regular visitors do.

　　瀧乃湯因為歷史悠久所以其日式建築與當今很多的大型溫泉會館比較下是很獨特的。這裡有分男女浴池，瀧乃湯裡自然形成的浴池，其歷史性是很吸引人的，還有，這裡的價格非常的平價，這樣的平價會讓你和當地人一樣會想定期的去泡湯。

此部分為**聽、讀雙效「填空」練習**，現在就一起動身，開始聽「短段落」，提升常考字彙、語感等答題能力！

Imagine 1._____ at a naturally formed hot springs 2._____ with steam rising from 3._____ below in cold 4._____. Sounds like Heaven! In 5._____, the Japanese built the first hot springs 6._____ in Taiwan called "Tengu Um house" in Bei Tou. They wanted to provide a place for the Japanese 7._____ similar to the hot springs bath they had at 8._____. It is still in 9._____ after all these years, but the name has changed to "Takimoto". A small 10._____ stands in the front yard to 11._____ the visit from the Crown Prince of Japan in 1923. Since it was built by Japanese, the 12._____ is quite unique when compared with the other 13._____ spa hotels in the area. In "Takimoto", there are 14._____ baths for men and 15._____. The naturally formed hot springs bath is very 16._____ to the visitors 17._____. Plus the low fee makes you want to return like the local 18._____ visitors do.

▶▶ 參考答案

1. soaking	2. pool
3. valley	4. weather
5. 1896	6. hotel
7. soldiers	8. home
9. business	10. monument
11. commemorate	12. architecture
13. large	14. separated
15. women	16. attractive
17. historically	18. regular

❶ hot springs: a naturally formed hot springs pool with the ____

    _____

❷ hot springs: the gas generating from the valley in cold _____

    _____

❸ Tengu Um house: a _____ built by the Japanese

❹ objective: provide the Japanese _____ with a place

❺ A small _____ stood in the front yard

❻ 1923: a _____ paid a visit here

❼ The _____ is known for its uniqueness.

❽ baths: In "Takimoto", men and women get to use the _____

    _____ room.

❶ steam

❷ weather

❸ hotel

❹ soldiers

❺ monument

❻ prince

❼ architecture

❽ individual

知本溫泉

Jhihben Hot Springs

▶▶ 影子跟讀「短段落」練習 🎧 MP3 028

此篇為**「影子跟讀短段落練習」**，規劃了由聽**「短段落」**的 shadowing 練習，強化聽力專注力和掌握各個考點！

Nestled in the Central Mountains, surrounded by metamorphic slate, in the middle of nature, is the Jhihben hot springs in Beinan Township in Taitung. Many think "Jhihben" was named by the Japanese, but "Jhihben" is originally from the aboriginal word "Kadibu" which sounded like "Jhihben", "Dibun" in the Taiwanese dialect.

知本溫泉位於臺灣臺東縣卑南鄉，知本溫泉屬於位於中央山脈板岩區的變質岩區溫泉。很多臺灣人以為「知本」是由日人所命名，但是「知本」其實是原住民語「卡地布」（Kadibu），臺語中聽起來就有點像是「知本」（Dibun）。

Aboriginal people found the Jhihben hot springs a long time ago, but during the Japanese occupation in Taiwan, they constructed some public bathhouses and hotels in the area. The Jhihben hot springs water temperature can get up to 95℃ with the pH value of around pH 8.5. The water contains bicarbonate ions around 627-1816 ppm and sodium ions of about 419-951 ppm. It is a neutral sodium bicarbonate spring. Colorless and odorless, the mineral springs are a pleasant way to enjoy the beautiful mountain scenery.

　　當地的原住民在很早以前就發現了知本溫泉，日本人只是在日據時代在這裡建設公共澡堂與賓館。知本溫泉的水溫最高可達 95℃，酸鹼值約 pH 8.5，含碳酸氫根離子約 627-1816 ppm，鈉離子約 419-951 ppm，屬於中性碳酸氫鈉泉。無色無味，這樣的溫泉是享受美麗山林風景的絕妙方式。

　　此部分為**聽、讀雙效「填空」練習**，現在就一起動身，開始聽「短段落」，提升常考字彙、語感等答題能力！

　　Nestled in the Central Mountains, 1.＿＿＿＿＿＿＿＿ by metamorphic slate, in the middle of 2.＿＿＿＿＿＿＿＿, is the Jhihben hot springs in Beinan Township in Taitung. Many think "Jhihben" was 3.＿＿＿＿＿＿＿＿ by the Japanese, but "Jhihben" is originally from the 4.＿＿＿＿＿＿＿＿ word "Kadibu" which sounded like "Jhihben", "Dibun" in the Taiwanese 5.＿＿＿＿＿＿＿＿.

　　Aboriginal 6.＿＿＿＿＿＿＿＿ found the Jhihben hot springs a long time ago, but during the Japanese 7.＿＿＿＿＿＿＿＿ in Taiwan, they 8.＿＿＿＿＿＿＿＿ some public bathhouses and 9.＿＿＿＿＿＿＿＿ in the area. The Jhihben hot springs water 10.＿＿＿＿＿＿＿＿ can get up to 95℃ with the pH 11.＿＿＿＿＿＿＿＿ of around pH 12.＿＿＿＿＿＿＿＿. The water 13.＿＿＿＿＿＿＿＿ bicarbonate ions around 627-1816 ppm and 14.＿＿＿＿＿＿＿＿ ions of about 419-951 ppm. It is a 15.＿＿＿＿＿＿＿＿ sodium bicarbonate spring. Colorless and 16.＿＿＿＿＿＿＿＿, the mineral springs are a 17.＿＿＿＿＿＿＿＿ way to enjoy the beautiful mountain 18.＿＿＿＿＿＿＿＿.

▶▶ 參考答案

1. surrounded	2. nature
3. named	4. aboriginal
5. dialect	6. people
7. occupation	8. constructed
9. hotels	10. temperature
11. value	12. 8.5
13. contains	14. sodium
15. neutral	16. odorless
17. pleasant	18. scenery

❶ the Jhihben hot springs: with the geology of the metamorphic

_____

❷ "Jhihben" is originally from the _____ word "Kadibu".

❸ "Dibun" in the Taiwanese _____.

❹ during occupation: they constructed some public _____ _____ and hotels

❺ water temperature: _____ degrees

❻ pH value: about pH _____

❼ bicarbonate ions: _____ ppm

❽ sodium ions: _____ ppm

❶ slate

❷ aboriginal

❸ dialect

❹ bathhouses

❺ 95

❻ 8.5

❼ 627-1816

❽ 419-951

礁溪溫泉
Jaiosi Hot Springs

▶▶ **影子跟讀「短段落」練習** 🎧 MP3 029

此篇為**「影子跟讀短段落練習」**，規劃了由聽**「短段落」**的 shadowing 練習，強化聽力專注力和掌握各個考點！

Get back to nature by visiting one of the best hot springs, Jaiosi, in Ilan. Because of special geological formations, it is a rare ground level hot springs. The rising steam from the underground heat joins with the ground water leaving a water so pure that it has multiple uses. The hot springs water is clear and odorless and has a neutral quality pH value between 7.2–7.9.

宜蘭礁溪最好的溫泉可以讓你感覺環繞在自然的懷抱裡。宜蘭礁溪因為特殊的地質構造，成為少見的平地溫泉。因為地下有熱源，上升的熱氣結合地下水之後產生多用途的泉水，這裡的溫泉青色無味，水質呈中性，pH 值在 7.2–7.9 之間。

The average water temperature is 50 degrees Celsius. The hot springs are not only used for spa and regular bath, after water treatment, the hot spring water here is also drinkable. Because it is ground level hot springs, visitors don't have to go all the way up to the mountains to enjoy the valley hot springs. The smart people of Ilan also use this type of neutral water to grow vegetables, make water drinkable, and to develop a unique aqua-culture industry.

　　平均水溫約在攝氏 50 度。礁溪的泉水不僅可以供作泡溫泉，洗澡的用途，在經過處理後也可以當礦泉水飲用，也因為是平地溫泉，更是讓人覺得不需翻山越嶺就可以享受到溫泉。而聰明的宜蘭人也利用這樣的中性的水質發展出很特別的溫泉蔬菜、可供飲用的溫泉水、以及溫泉養殖的產業。

　　此部分為**聽、讀雙效「填空」練習**，現在就一起動身，開始聽「短段落」，提升常考字彙、語感等答題能力！

　　Get back to 1.＿＿＿＿＿＿ by visiting one of the best hot springs, Jaiosi, in Ilan. Because of special 2.＿＿＿＿＿＿ formations, it is a 3.＿＿＿＿＿＿ ground level hot springs. The rising 4.＿＿＿＿＿＿ from the 5.＿＿＿＿＿＿ heat joins with the ground water leaving a water so 6.＿＿＿＿＿＿ that it has 7.＿＿＿＿＿ uses. The hot springs water is clear and 8.＿＿＿＿＿ and has a neutral quality pH value between 7.2–7.9. The 9.＿＿＿＿＿ water temperature is 50 degrees 10.＿＿＿＿＿. The hot springs are not only used for spa and 11.＿＿＿＿＿ bath, after water 12.＿＿＿＿＿, the hot spring water here is also 13.＿＿＿＿＿. Because it is 14.＿＿＿＿＿ level hot springs, visitors don't have to go all the way up to the mountains to enjoy the 15.＿＿＿＿＿ hot springs. The smart people of Ilan also use this type of neutral water to grow 16.＿＿＿＿＿, make water drinkable, and to 17.＿＿＿＿＿ a unique 18.＿＿＿＿＿ industry.

▶▶ 參考答案

1. nature	2. geological
3. rare	4. steam
5. underground	6. pure
7. multiple	8. odorless
9. average	10. Celsius
11. regular	12. treatment
13. drinkable	14. ground
15. valley	16. vegetables
17. develop	18. aquaculture

Part 1 生活類主題

Part 2 學術類主題

❶ Jaiosi: contains special _____ formations

❷ Jaiosi: it is a rare _____ level hot springs.

❸ steam: is generated from underground _____

❹ the water: clear and _____

❺ the water: has a _____ quality pH value

❻ average water temperature: _____ degrees Celsius

❼ Before water treatment, the hot spring water here is _____ _____ .

❽ other use: neutral water to cultivate _____

❶ geological

❷ ground

❸ heat

❹ odorless

❺ neutral

❻ 50

❼ undrinkable

❽ vegetables

UNIT **30**

拉拉山水蜜桃

▶▶ 影子跟讀「短段落」練習 🎧 MP3 030

　　此篇為**「影子跟讀短段落練習」**，規劃了由聽**「短段落」**的 shadowing 練習，強化聽力專注力和掌握各個考點！

　　If you're visiting Taoyuan in June or July, make sure you try Lalashan's famous peaches. They are incredibly sweet and juicy. While there, take a hike among the ancient cypress trees in the Lalashan Nature Reserves. The Sacred Tree Grove is full of natural red cypress trees that range in age from 500 years old to nearly 3,000. In the late autumn, the leaves change from green to red. It is very colorful and attractive. Only the 30 hectares that contain the ancient cypress grove are open to visitors while the rest of the reserve is set aside for ecological conservation.

　　當你在六月中至七月底去桃園玩，你一定要試試拉拉山出名的水蜜桃。拉拉山的水蜜桃香甜多汁。拉拉山自然保護區內有很多巨大的神木，其天然紅檜巨木林樹齡約在 500 年至 3,000 年左右，每到深秋，園內變色植物由綠轉紅，五顏六色非常吸引人。拉拉山自然保護區並未全面開放遊客參觀，僅開放以神木群為主的地區約 30 公頃。

This area is an important ecological conservation area in Taiwan with many rare wild animals, such as the Formosan black bear, macaques, and muntjac deer. Bird watchers come here to spot the diverse and unique bird species.

拉拉山自然保護區內有很多難得一見的野生動物，如臺灣黑熊、彌猴、山羌等，是臺灣生態保育的重要地方，賞鳥者會到這裡來看種類繁多的獨特鳥類。

　　此部分為**聽、讀雙效「填空」練習**，現在就一起動身，開始聽「短段落」，提升常考字彙、語感等答題能力！

　　If you're visiting Taoyuan in 1.＿＿＿＿＿＿＿ or 2.＿＿＿＿＿＿, make sure you try Lalashan's famous 3.＿＿＿＿＿＿＿. They are 4.＿＿＿＿＿＿＿ sweet and juicy. While there, take a 5.＿＿＿＿＿＿ among the 6.＿＿＿＿＿＿＿ cypress trees in the Lalashan Nature 7.＿＿＿＿＿＿＿. The Sacred Tree Grove is full of natural red cypress trees that 8.＿＿＿＿＿＿＿ in age from 500 years old to nearly 9.＿＿＿＿＿＿. In the late 10.＿＿＿＿＿＿＿, the leaves change from 11.＿＿＿＿＿＿＿ to red. It is very colorful and 12.＿＿＿＿＿＿＿. Only the 30 hectares that contain the ancient cypress 13.＿＿＿＿＿＿ are open to visitors while the rest of the reserve is set aside for 14.＿＿＿＿＿＿ conservation.

　　This area is an important ecological conservation area in Taiwan with many rare wild 15.＿＿＿＿＿＿＿, such as the Formosan black bear, 16.＿＿＿＿＿＿, and muntjac 17.＿＿＿＿＿＿＿. Bird 18.＿＿＿＿＿＿ come here to spot the diverse and unique bird species.

▶▶ 參考答案

1. June	2. July
3. peaches	4. incredibly
5. hike	6. ancient
7. Reserves	8. range
9. 3,000	10. autumn
11. green	12. attractive
13. grove	14. ecological
15. animals	16. macaques
17. deer	18. watchers

❶ product: renowned for its _____

❷ Nature Reserves: go _____ among the ancient cypress trees

❸ The Sacred Tree Grove: contains natural _____ cypress trees

❹ autumn: the leaves change from _____ to red

❺ visiting: visitors are allowed to see only _____ hectares

❻ the rest: is kept for _____ conservation

❼ rare wild animals: such as the Formosan black _____, macaques, and muntjac _____

❽ The _____ of bird species attracts bird watchers.

❶ peaches

❷ hiking

❸ red

❹ green

❺ 30

❻ ecological

❼ bear, deer

❽ diversity

掌握聽力和閱讀中循環出現的學術類主題，例如紙的發明等等，並記憶相關主題的字彙，最後輔以三個階段的聽力練習，迅速攻略雅思聽力 section 3 和 section 4。

PART 2

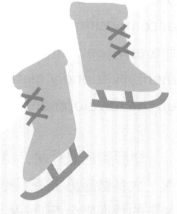

塑膠工業之父

此篇為**「影子跟讀短段落練習」**，規劃了由聽「**短段落**」的 shadowing 練習，強化聽力專注力和掌握各個考點！

What is plastics exactly? The majority of the polymers are based on chains of carbon atoms alone with oxygen, sulfur, or nitrogen. Most plastics contain other organic or inorganic compounds blended in. The number of additives ranges from zero percentage to more than 50% for certain electronic applications. The invention of plastic was not only a great success but also brought us a serious environmental concern regarding its slow decomposition rate after being discarded. One way to help with the environment is to practice recycling or use other environmentally friendly materials instead. Another approach is to speed up the development of biodegradable plastic.

塑膠到底是什麼？大多數聚合物都基於碳原子和氧、硫、或氮的鏈。大多數塑膠混有其他有機或無機化合物。在一些電子應用上，添加劑的量從零至 50%以上。塑膠的發明獲得了巨大的成功，但也給我們帶來了關於其被丟棄後緩慢分解所造成嚴重的環境問題。練習回收

或改用其他對環境友好的材料是幫助環境的一種方法。另一種方法是，加快生物分解性塑料的開發。

The father of the Plastics Industry, Leo Baekeland, was born in Belgium on November 14th, 1863. He was best known for his invention of Bakelite which is an inexpensive, nonflammable and versatile plastic. Because of his invention, the plastic industry started to bloom and became a popular material in many different industries.

塑膠工業之父，利奧‧貝克蘭，於 1863 年 11 月 14 日出生於比利時。他最為人知的是酚醛塑的發明，這是一種廉價，不可燃和通用的塑膠。由於他的發明，塑料行業開始盛行，在許多不同的行業成為一個受歡迎的材料。

此部分為**聽、讀雙效「填空」練習**，現在就一起動身，開始聽「短段落」，提升常考字彙、語感等答題能力！

What is plastics exactly? The majority of the 1.＿＿＿＿＿ are based on chains of 2.＿＿＿＿＿ alone with 3.＿＿＿＿＿＿＿, sulfur, or 4.＿＿＿＿＿. Most plastics contain other organic or 5.＿＿＿＿＿ blended in. The number of 6.＿＿＿＿＿ ranges from 7.＿＿＿＿＿ percentage to more than 50% for certain 8.＿＿＿＿＿. The 9.＿＿＿＿＿ of plastic was not only a great 10.＿＿＿＿＿ but also brought us a serious 11.＿＿＿＿＿ concern regarding its 12.＿＿＿＿＿ rate after being discarded. One way to help with the environment is to practice 13.＿＿＿＿＿ or use other 14.＿＿＿＿＿ materials instead. Another approach is to speed up the development of 15.＿＿＿＿＿. The father of the Plastics Industry, Leo Baekeland, was born in 16.＿＿＿＿＿ on November 14th, 1863. He was best known for his invention of 17.＿＿＿＿＿ which is an inexpensive, 18.＿＿＿＿＿ and versatile plastic. Because of his invention, the plastic industry started to 19.＿＿＿＿＿ and became a popular material in many different 20.＿＿＿＿＿.

▶▶ 參考答案

1. polymers
2. carbon atoms
3. oxygen
4. nitrogen
5. inorganic compounds
6. additives
7. zero
8. electronic applications
9. invention
10. success
11. environmental
12. slow decomposition
13. recycling
14. environmentally friendly
15. biodegradable plastic
16. Belgium
17. Bakelite
18. nonflammable
19. bloom
20. industries

❶ polymers: chains of carbon atoms alone with _____, sulfur, or _____.

❷ Most plastics: contain other organic or inorganic _____

___

❸ electronic applications: _____ ranges from zero percentage to more than 50%

❹ invention of plastic: there is a serious _____ concern.

❺ plastic: delaying _____

❻ help: practice _____ or use products beneficial to the environment

❼ other approach: hasten the development of _____ plastic

❽ Leo Baekeland: was given birth in _____

❶ oxygen, nitrogen

❷ compounds

❸ additives

❹ environmental

❺ decomposition

❻ recycling

❼ biodegradable

❽ Belgium

UNIT 32

諾貝爾的生平

▶▶ 影子跟讀「短段落」練習 🎧 MP3 032

　　此篇為「**影子跟讀短段落練習**」，規劃了由聽「**短段落**」的 shadowing 練習，強化聽力專注力和掌握各個考點！

　　Nobel was born in Stockholm, Sweden on October 21st, 1833. His family moved to St. Petersburg in Russia in 1842. Nobel was sent to private tutoring, and he excelled in his studies, particularly in chemistry and languages. He achieved fluency in English, French, German and Russian. Throughout his life, Nobel only went to school for 18 months. In 1860, Nobel started his invention of dynamite, and it was 1866 when he first invented dynamite successfully. Nobel never let himself take any rest. He founded Nitroglycerin AB in Stockholm, Sweden in 1864.

　　諾貝爾於 1833 年 10 月 21 日出生在瑞典斯德哥爾摩。在 1842 年時，他舉家遷往俄羅斯聖彼得堡。諾貝爾被送往私塾，他擅長於學習，特別是在化學和語言。他能精通英語，法語，德語和俄語。終其一生，諾貝爾只去了學校 18 個月。1860 年，諾貝爾開始了炸藥的發明。1866 年，他第一次成功地發明了炸藥。諾貝爾從來沒有讓自己休息。他於 1864 年在瑞典斯德哥爾摩創立硝酸甘油 AB 公司。

A year later, he built the Alfred Nobel Co. Factory in Hamburg, Germany. In 1866, he established the United States Blasting Oil Company in the U.S. And 4 years later, he established the Société général pour la fabrication de la dynamite in Paris, France. Nobel was proud to say he is a world citizen. He passed away in 1896. A year before that, he started the Nobel prize which is awarded yearly to people whose work helps humanity. When he died, Alfred Nobel left behind a nine million- dollar endowment fund.

一年後，他在德國漢堡建立了阿爾弗雷德・諾貝爾公司的工廠。1866 年，他在美國成立了美國爆破石油公司。4 年後，他又在法國巴黎成立了炸藥實驗室。諾貝爾自豪地説，他是一個世界公民。他在 1896 年過世。在他過世前，他成立諾貝爾獎以鼓勵對人類有幫助的人們 。當他過世時，諾貝爾留下了九百萬美元的捐贈基金。

此部分為**聽、讀雙效「填空」練習**，現在就一起動身，開始聽「短段落」，提升常考字彙、語感等答題能力！

Nobel was born in Stockholm, 1._____ on 2._____
_____, 1833. His family moved to St. Petersburg in 3._____
_____ in 1842. Nobel was sent to 4._____, and he excelled in his studies, particularly in 5._____ and languages. He achieved fluency in English, French, 6._____
__.

Throughout his life, Nobel only went to school for 7._____
_____. In 1860, Nobel started his invention of 8._____,
and it was 1866 when he first invented the 9._____.
Nobel never let himself take any rest. He founded Nitroglycerin
AB in Stockholm, Sweden in 1864.

A year later, he built the Alfred Nobel Co. Factory in Hamburg, Germany. In 1866, he established the United States Blasting 10._____ in the U.S. And 4 years later, he established the Société général pour la fabrication de la dynamite in
Paris, France. Nobel was proud to say he is a world citizen. He
passed away in 1896. A year before that, he started the 11.____
_____ which is awarded yearly to people whose 12._____
_____ helps 13._____. When he died, Alfred Nobel
left behind a nine million- dollar 14._____.

▶▶ 參考答案

1. Sweden	2. October 21st
3. Russia	4. private tutoring
5. chemistry	6. German and Russian
7. 18 months	8. dynamite
9. dynamite successfully	10. Oil Company
11. Nobel prize	12. work
13. humanity	14. endowment fund

❶ Nobel: moved to St. Petersburg in _____ in 1842

❷ subject: especially in _____ and languages

❸ language aptitude: fluency in multiple languages, including English, French, German and _____.

❹ study: _____ months

❺ invention: _____

❻ Nobel: he is a _____ citizen

❼ the Nobel prize: a prize for the person who contributes to __ _____

❽ left behind an endowment _____

❶ Russia

❷ chemistry

❸ Russian

❹ 18

❺ dynamite

❻ world

❼ humanity

❽ fund

直升機的發展和貢獻

此篇為「**影子跟讀短段落練習**」，規劃了由聽「**短段落**」的 shadowing 練習，強化聽力專注力和掌握各個考點！

Since then, the helicopter development was going on all over the world, from the United States, to England, France, Denmark and even Russia. But it was not until 1942 that a helicopter designed by Igor Sikorsky reached a full-scale production. The most common helicopter configuration had a single main rotor with an antitorque tail rotor, unlike the earlier designs that had multiple rotors. Centuries of development later, the invention of helicopter improves the transportation of people and cargo, uses for military, construction, firefighting, research, rescue, medical transport, and many others. The contributions of the helicopter are uncountable.

此後，直升機在世界各地不停的發展，有來自美國、英國、法國、丹麥，甚至俄羅斯。直到 1942 年由伊戈爾·西科斯基設計的直升機才達到全面性的生產。最常見的直升機配置有具有抗扭矩尾槳和單一主螺旋槳。不同於早期的設計，有多個螺旋槳。幾個世紀的發展

之後，直升機的發明提高了人員和貨物的運輸，使用於軍事、建築、消防、科研、救護，醫療轉運，和許多其他地方。直升機的貢獻是不可數計的。

Some people might recognize the name of Igor Ivanovich Sikorsky from the public airport in Fairfield County, Connecticut. No doubt that due to the great contributions from Sikorsky to the aviation industry, the airport of his hometown decided to be named after him.

有些人可能會從康乃狄克州費爾菲爾德縣的大眾機場那裡認出「伊戈爾・伊万諾維奇・西科斯基」這個名字。毫無疑問的，由於西科斯基對航空業的巨大貢獻，家鄉的機場決定以他的名字來命名。

Part 1 生活類主題

Part 2 學術類主題

　　此部分為**聽、讀雙效「填空」練習**，現在就一起動身，開始聽「短段落」，提升常考字彙、語感等答題能力！

　　Since then, the 1._____ development was going on all over the world, from the 2._____, to England, France, 3._____ and even Russia. But it was not until 1942 that a helicopter designed by Igor Sikorsky reached a 4._____. The most common helicopter 5._____ had a single main rotor with an antitorque tail rotor, unlike the 6._____ that had multiple rotors. Centuries of development later, the invention of helicopter improves the 7._____ of people and 8._____, uses for 9._____, construction, 10._____, research, rescue, 11._____, and many others. The 12._____ of the helicopter are uncountable.

　　Some people might recognize the name of Igor Ivanovich Sikorsky from the public airport in Fairfield County, 13._____. No doubt that due to the great contributions from Sikorsky to the 14._____, the 15._____ of his 16._____ decided to be named after him.

▶▶ 參考答案

1. helicopter
2. United States
3. Denmark
4. full-scale production
5. configuration
6. earlier designs
7. transportation
8. cargo
9. military
10. firefighting
11. medical transport
12. contributions
13. Connecticut
14. aviation industry
15. airport
16. hometown

Part 1 生活類主題

Part 2 學術類主題

❶ development: in various countries, even _____

❷ Igor Sikorsky: a full-scale _____

❸ The most common helicopter _____ had a single main rotor

❹ invention: improves the transportation of people and _____ _____

❺ other uses: military, construction, firefighting, _____, rescue, medical transport, and many others.

❻ The contributions of the helicopter are _____.

❼ recognition: from the public _____

❽ contributions: the _____ industry

❶ Russia

❷ production

❸ configuration

❹ cargo

❺ research

❻ uncountable

❼ airport

❽ aviation

聽診器帶來的便利性

此篇為「**影子跟讀短段落練習**」，規劃了由聽「**短段落**」的 shadowing 練習，強化聽力專注力和掌握各個考點！

Graduating in medicine in 1804, Laennec became an associate at the Societe de IEcole de Medicine. He then found that tubercle lesions could be present in all organs of the body and not just the lungs. By 1816, at the age of 35, he was offered the position of a physician at the Necker Hospital in Paris. Laennec is considered to be one of the greatest doctors of all time. It was him that introduced auscultation. This method involves listening and identifying various sounds made by different body organs.

1804 年畢業於醫學系，拉埃內克成為 Societe de IEcole de Medicine 的一員。之後他發現了結節性病變可能存在於身體的所有器官，而不僅僅是肺部。到了 1816 年，在他 35 歲的時候，他得到了巴黎內克爾醫院醫生的位子。拉埃內克被認為是所有時代內最偉大的醫生之一。他引進了聽診技術。這種方法涉及聽力，並確定由不同的身體器官製成各種聲音。

Before the invention of this method, doctors needed to put their ears on patients' chests to diagnose patients' problems. He felt uncomfortable especially while he was diagnosing young women. This led to the innovation of a new device called the stethoscope which he initially termed as "chest examiner". With stethoscope, nowadays all doctors are able to study different sounds of heart and understand patients' condition in a much more precise way. Laennec's works were way ahead of his times and he had a great impact on medical science.

　　這種方法發明之前，醫生需要把耳朵放在患者的胸前以診斷病人的問題。由其當他診斷年輕女性時，這個方法令他不舒服這促使了一個新的設備的發明，稱為聽診器。他最初稱這個儀器為「胸部測試器」。因為聽診器，現在所有的醫生都能夠學習心臟的不同的聲音，並以一個更精確的方式了解患者的病情。拉埃內克的作品於是遙遙領先了他所處的時代並對醫學有很大的影響。

　　此部分為**聽、讀雙效「填空」練習**，現在就一起動身，開始聽「短段落」，提升常考字彙、語感等答題能力！

　　Graduating in 1.＿＿＿＿＿＿ in 1804, Laennec became 2.＿＿＿＿＿＿ at the Societe de lEcole de Medicine. He then found that tubercle lesions could be present in all 3.＿＿＿＿＿＿ of the body and not just the 4.＿＿＿＿＿＿. By 1816, at the age of 5.＿＿＿＿＿＿, he was offered the position of a physician at the Necker 6.＿＿＿＿＿＿. Laennec is considered to be one of the greatest 7.＿＿＿＿＿＿ of all time. It was him that introduced 8.＿＿＿＿＿＿. This method involves 9.＿＿＿＿＿＿ and identifying 10.＿＿＿＿＿＿ made by different body organs.

　　Before the invention of this method, doctors needed to put their ears on 11.＿＿＿＿＿＿ to diagnose patients' problems. He felt uncomfortable especially while he was diagnosing 12.＿＿＿＿＿＿. This led to the 13.＿＿＿＿＿＿ of a new device called the 14.＿＿＿＿＿＿ which he initially termed as "chest examiner". With stethoscope, nowadays all doctors are able to study different 15.＿＿＿＿＿＿ and understand patients' condition in a much more precise way. Laennec's works were way ahead of his times and he had a great impact on 16.＿＿＿＿＿＿.

▶▶ 參考答案

1. medicine	2. an associate
3. organs	4. lungs
5. 35	6. Hospital in Paris
7. doctors	8. auscultation
9. listening	10. various sounds
11. patients' chests	12. young women
13. innovation	14. stethoscope
15. sounds of heart	16. medical science

❶ Laennec: has a degree in _____

❷ finding: not just the _____

❸ age of 35: he was offered the _____ of a physician

❹ auscultation: involves listening and identifying various _____

_____

❺ Before the invention: doctors needed to put their ears on patients' _____

❻ discomfort: while diagnosing young _____

❼ stethoscope: initially termed as "chest _____ "

❽ impact: on _____ science

❶ medicine

❷ lungs

❸ position

❹ sounds

❺ chests

❻ women

❼ examiner

❽ medical

UNIT 35

汽車發展史

▶▶ 影子跟讀「短段落」練習 🎧 MP3 035

　　此篇為**「影子跟讀短段落練習」**，規劃了由聽**「短段落」**的 shadowing 練習，強化聽力專注力和掌握各個考點！

　　There were many people who made a great contribution to the invention of different types of automobiles. But it was only when Karl Benz built the first petrol automobile that vehicles became practical and went into actual production. The first gasoline-powered automobile built by Karl Benz contained an internal combustion engine. He built it in 1885 in Mannheim and was granted a patent for his automobile in 1886. Two years later, he began the first production of automobiles. In 1889, Gottlied Daimler and Wilhelm Maybach also designed a vehicle from scratch in Stuttgart.

　　許多人都曾對發明不同類型的汽車有偉大的貢獻，但直到卡爾・賓士製造了第一台汽油汽車，汽車才真正能被有效利用，走進實際生產。卡爾・賓士製作了第一個汽油動力汽車內所用的內燃機。他於 1885 年製作，並在 1886 年於曼海姆取得第一台汽車的專利。2 年後他開始了第一輛汽車的生產。1889 年，古特蘭・戴姆勒和威廉・邁

巴赫也在斯圖加特開始了汽車的設計。

In 1895, a British engineer, Frederick William Lanchester built the first four-wheeled petrol driven automobile and also patented the disc brake. Between 1895 and 1898, the first electric starter was installed in the Benz Velo. By the 1930s, most of the mechanical technology used in today's automobiles had been invented. But due to the Great Depression, the number of auto manufacturers declined sharply. Many companies consolidated and matured. After that, the automobile market was booming for decades until the 1970s.

1895 年，一名英國工程師，腓特烈・威廉在曼徹斯特製造了第一台四輪驅動的汽油汽車，並申請了盤式制動器的專利。在 1895 年和 1898 年間，賓士在車內安裝了首款的電動起動器。到了 1930 年代，今天汽車內使用的大部分機械技術已被發明出來。但由於經濟大蕭條，汽車製造業的數量急劇下降。許多公司合併且趨於成熟。在此之後，汽車市場蓬勃發展了幾十年直到 70 年代。

此部分為**聽、讀雙效「填空」練習**，現在就一起動身，開始聽「短段落」，提升常考字彙、語感等答題能力！

There were many people who made a great 1._____ to the invention of different types of 2._____. But it was only when Karl Benz built the first 3._____ that vehicles became practical and went into 4._____. The first 5._____ automobile built by Karl Benz contained an 6._____. He built it in 1885 in Mannheim and was granted 7._____ for his automobile in 1886. Two years later, he began the first production of automobiles. In 1889, Gottlied Daimler and Wilhelm Maybach also designed a vehicle from 8._____ in Stuttgart.

In 1895, a 9._____, Frederick William Lanchester built the first 10._____ petrol driven automobile and also patented the disc brake. Between 1895 and 1898, the first electric starter was installed in the Benz Velo. By the 1930s, most of the 11._____ used in today's automobiles had been invented. But due to the 12._____, the number of auto manufacturers declined sharply. Many 13._____ consolidated and matured. After that, the automobile 14._____ was booming for decades until the 1970s.

▶▶ 參考答案

1. contribution	2. automobiles
3. petrol automobile	4. actual production
5. gasoline-powered	6. internal combustion engine
7. a patent	8. scratch
9. British engineer	10. fourwheeled
11. mechanical technology	12. Great Depression
13. companies	14. market

① Karl Benz: built the first _____ automobile

② first gasoline-powered automobile: contained an internal combustion _____

③ 1886: was granted a _____ for his automobile

④ 1888: began the first _____ of automobiles

⑤ 1895: patented the disc _____

⑥ Between 1895 and 1898: the first electric _____ was installed

⑦ the Great Depression: the number of auto _____ decreased considerably

⑧ after 1970s: the market experienced a _____

❶ petrol

❷ engine

❸ patent

❹ production

❺ brake

❻ starter

❼ manufacturers

❽ boom

飛機的發明

▶▶ **影子跟讀「短段落」練習** 🎧 MP3 036

　　此篇為 **「影子跟讀短段落練習」**，規劃了由聽 **「短段落」** 的 shadowing 練習，強化聽力專注力和掌握各個考點！

　　According to the document from IATA in 2011, 2.8 billion passengers were carried by airplane, which means on average there are 690,000 passengers in the air at any given moment. Air travel is known as the safest way to travel and it shortens the distance between countries. How would the world be today without the invention of airplanes? We would never know. The first airplane was invented by Orville and Wilbur Wright in 1903.

　　據國際航空運輸協會在 2011 年的文件指出，一年中一共有 28 億的乘客搭乘飛機，這意味著無論任何時候都有平均 69 萬位乘客在空中飛行。航空旅行號稱是最安全的旅行方式，它縮短了國與國之間的距離。如果沒有飛機的發明，今天這個世界會變如何？我們永遠不會知道。

　　Before the Wright's invention, many people made numerous

attempts to fly like birds. In 1799, Sir George Cayley designed the first fixed-wing aircraft. In 1874, Felix duTemple made the first attempt at powered flight by hopping off the end of a ramp in a steam-driven monoplane.

在奧維爾和威爾，萊特於 1903 年發明第一架飛機以前，很多人嘗試了像鳥一樣的飛翔方式。1799 年，喬治‧凱利爵士設計了第一架固定翼的飛機。1874 年，菲利克斯‧杜湯普跳躍過斜坡，利用蒸汽驅動單翼，第一次嘗試動力飛行。

In 1894, the first controlled flight was made by Otto Lilienthal by shifting his body weight. Inspired by Lilienthal, the Wright brothers experimented with aerodynamic surfaces to control an airplane in flight and later on made the first airplane that was powered and controllable.

1894 年，奧托‧李林塔爾利用轉移他的體重，創造出第一架可控飛行機。由於李林塔爾的啟發，萊特兄弟實驗氣動表面來控制飛行的飛機，後來提出電動並可控制的第一架飛機。

此部分為**聽、讀雙效「填空」練習**，現在就一起動身，開始聽「短段落」，提升常考字彙、語感等答題能力！

According to the 1.＿＿＿＿＿＿＿ from IATA in 2011, 2.＿＿＿＿＿＿＿＿＿ were carried by airplane, which means on average there are 3.＿＿＿＿＿＿＿ in the air at any given moment. 4.＿＿＿＿＿＿＿ is known as the safest way to travel and it shortens the distance between 5.＿＿＿＿＿＿＿. How would the world be today without the invention of 6.＿＿＿＿＿＿＿? We would never know. The first airplane was invented by Orville and Wilbur Wright in 1903.

Before the Wright's invention, many people made 7.＿＿＿＿＿＿＿ to fly like 8.＿＿＿＿＿＿＿. In 1799, Sir George Cayley designed the first 9.＿＿＿＿＿＿＿. In 1874, Felix duTemple made the first attempt at powered flight by hopping off the end of a ramp in a steam-driven 10.＿＿＿＿＿＿＿.

In 1894, the first controlled flight was made by Otto Lilienthal by shifting his 11.＿＿＿＿＿＿＿. Inspired by Lilienthal, the Wright brothers experimented with aerodynamic 12.＿＿＿＿＿＿＿ to control 13.＿＿＿＿＿＿＿ in flight and later on made the first airplane that was powered and 14.＿＿＿＿＿＿＿.

▶▶ 參考答案

1. document	2. 2.8 billion passengers
3. 690,000 passengers	4. Air travel
5. countries	6. airplanes
7. numerous attempts	8. birds
9. fixed-wing aircraft	10. monoplane
11. body weight	12. surfaces
13. an airplane	14. controllable

❶ IATA: _____ billion passengers were carried by airplane

❷ air travel: on average _____ passengers

❸ air travel: shortens the _____ between countries

❹ invention: invented by Orville and Wilbur Wright in _____ _____

❺ 1799: designed the first fixed-wing _____

❻ 1874: first attempt at powered flight by hopping off the end of a ramp in a steam-driven _____

❼ 1894: the first controlled flight was made by Otto Lilienthal by shifting his body _____

❽ inspiration: the Wright brothers experimented with aerodynamic _____

❶ 2.8

❷ 690,000

❸ distance

❹ 1903

❺ aircraft

❻ monoplane

❼ weight

❽ surfaces

利普斯
Lippershey

▶▶ 影子跟讀「短段落」練習 🎧 MP3 037

此篇為**「影子跟讀短段落練習」**，規劃了由聽**「短段落」**的 shadowing 練習，強化聽力專注力和掌握各個考點！

Hans Lippershey, a master lens grinder and spectacle maker was born in Wesel Germany in 1570. He then got married and settled in Middelburg in the Netherlands in 1594. Eight years later, he immigrated in the Netherlands. Lippershey filed a patent for the telescope in 1607 and this was known as the earliest written record of a refracting telescope. There are several different versions of how Lippershey came up with the invention of the telescope.

身為一位鏡片研磨師和眼鏡製造商的漢斯・利普斯在 1570 年誕生於德國韋塞爾。爾後，在 1594 年定居於荷蘭米德爾堡，並在同一年結婚。8 年後移民荷蘭。利普斯在 1607 年申請了望遠鏡的專利，這被稱為是折射望遠鏡最早的文字記錄。對於利普斯如何想出望遠鏡的原因有幾種不同的版本。

The most interesting one has to be in which Lippershey observed two kids playing with lenses and commented how they could make a far away weather-vane seem closer when looking at it through two lenses. Lippershey's original instrument consisted of either two convex lenses for an inverted image or a convex objective and a concave eyepiece lens so it would have an upright image. Lippershey remained in Middelburg until he passed away in 1619.

　　最有趣的版本是有一次利普斯觀察到兩個小孩玩耍時的對話，他們在評論如何利用鏡頭讓一個遙遠的天氣風向標看起來似乎更接近。利普斯的原始工具包括利用兩個凸透鏡以呈現出一個倒置的圖像，或利用凸物鏡和凹透鏡的眼鏡片以呈現出一個正面的圖像。利普斯終其一生留在米德爾，直到他在 1619 年去世。

此部分為**聽、讀雙效「填空」練習**，現在就一起動身，開始聽「短段落」，提升常考字彙、語感等答題能力！

Hans Lippershey, a master 1._____ and 2._____ _____ was born in Wesel 3._____ in 1570. He then got married and settled in Middelburg in the 4._____ in 1594. Eight years later, he immigrated in the Netherlands. Lippershey filed 5._____ for the 6._____ in 1607 and this was known as the earliest 7._____ of a refracting telescope. There are several different 8._____ of how Lippershey came up with the invention of the telescope.

The most interesting one has to be in which Lippershey observed 9._____ playing with lenses and commented how they could make a far away weather-vane seem closer when looking at it through 10._____. Lippershey's original 11._____ consisted of either 12._____ for an inverted image or a convex 13._____ and a 14._____ _____ eyepiece lens so it would have an 15._____. Lippershey remained in 16._____ until he passed away in 1619.

▶▶ 參考答案

1. lens grinder	2. spectacle maker
3. Germany	4. Netherlands
5. a patent	6. telescope
7. written record	8. versions
9. two kids	10. two lenses
11. instrument	12. two convex lenses
13. objective	14. concave
15. upright image	16. Middelburg

Part 1 生活類主題

Part 2 學術類主題

❶ Hans Lippershey: a _____ maker

❷ 1594: settled in Middelburg in the _____

❸ _____: he immigrated in the Netherlands.

❹ 1607: filed a patent for _____

❺ interesting version: came from an _____ on children

❻ comment: make a far away weather-vane seem closer when looking at it through _____ lenses

❼ original instrument: to get an _____ image

❽ _____: he passed away

❶ spectacle

❷ Netherlands

❸ 1602

❹ telescope

❺ observation

❻ two

❼ upright

❽ 1619

打字機的發明

▶▶ 影子跟讀「短段落」練習 🎧 MP3 038

　　此篇為「**影子跟讀短段落練習**」，規劃了由聽「**短段落**」的 shadowing 練習，強化聽力專注力和掌握各個考點！

　　A typewriter is a writing machine that has one character on each key press. The machine prints characters by making ink impressions on a moveable type letterpress printing. Typewriters, like other practical products, such as automobiles, telephones, and refrigerators, the invention was developed by numerous inventors. The very first record of the typewriter invention was back in 1575.

　　打字機是一個寫作的機器，在每個按鍵上各有一個字母。機器利用活字凸版印刷通過墨水打印字符。打字機，如同其他實用的產品，如汽車、電話和冰箱，是由眾多的發明人所開發出來的。打字機發明的第一個記錄最早在 1575 年。

　　In 1575, an Italian printmaker, Francesco Rampazzetto, invented the"scrittura tattile" which is a machine to impress letters on papers. Hundreds of years passed by and many different types of typewriters were being developed. However, no commercially practical machine was created. It wasn't until 1829 that an American inventor William Austin Burt patented a machine called the"Typographer" which is listed as the "first typewriter". However, the design was still not practical enough for the market since it was slower than handwriting. In 1865, Rasmus Malling-Hansen from Denmark invented the first commercially sold typewriter, called the Hansen Writing Ball. It was successfully sold in Europe. In the US, the first commercially successful typewriter was invented by Christopher Latham Sholes in 1868.

　　1575 年，意大利的版畫家，弗朗西斯，發明了「scritturatattile」，這是一台用來打字的機器。幾百年過去了，很多不同類型的打字機被開發出來。然而，沒有商業實用機的創建。直到 1829 年，美國發明家威廉‧奧斯汀伯特申請了一台機器的專利稱為「字體設計」，它被列為「第一台打字機」。然而，設計仍然不夠實用，因為它比寫字要緩慢。1865 年，來自丹麥的拉斯穆斯莫林‧漢森發明了第一台在市場上銷售的打字機，叫做漢森寫作球。它成功地在歐洲銷售。在美國，第一個商業成功的打字機是在 1868 年由克里斯托弗‧萊瑟姆‧肖爾斯所發明的。

此部分為**聽、讀雙效「填空」練習**，現在就一起動身，開始聽「短段落」，提升常考字彙、語感等答題能力！

A 1.＿＿＿＿＿＿＿ is a writing 2.＿＿＿＿＿＿＿ that has one character on each key press. The machine prints characters by making 3.＿＿＿＿＿＿＿ on a moveable type letterpress printing. Typewriters, like other 4.＿＿＿＿＿＿＿ such as automobiles , 5.＿＿＿＿＿＿＿ , and 6.＿＿＿＿＿＿＿, the invention was developed by numerous 7.＿＿＿＿＿＿＿. The very first record of the typewriter invention was back in 1575.

In 1575, an Italian printmaker, Francesco Rampazzetto, invented the "scrittura tattile" which is 8.＿＿＿＿＿＿＿ to impress letters on papers. Hundreds of years passed by and many different types of typewriters were being developed. However, no 9.＿＿＿＿＿＿＿ machine was created. It wasn't until 1829 that an 10.＿＿＿＿＿＿＿ William Austin Burt patented a machine called the "Typographer" which is listed as the "first typewriter". However, the 11.＿＿＿＿＿＿＿ was still not practical enough for the market since it was slower than 12.＿＿＿＿＿＿＿. In 1865, Rasmus Malling-Hansen from 13.＿＿＿＿＿＿＿ invented the first commercially sold typewriter, called the Hansen Writing Ball. It was successfully sold in 14.＿＿＿＿＿＿＿. In the US, the first commercially successful typewriter was invented by Christopher Latham Sholes in 1868.

▶▶ 參考答案

1. typewriter	2. machine
3. ink impressions	4. practical products
5. telephones	6. refrigerators
7. inventors	8. a machine
9. commercially practical	10. American inventor
11. design	12. handwriting
13. Denmark	14. Europe

Part 1 生活類主題

Part 2 學術類主題

❶ typewriter: is a writing _____

❷ prints characters: making ink _____ on a moveable type letterpress printing

❸ other practical products: include automobiles, telephones, and _____

❹ _____: the very first record

❺ the"Typographer": _____ for the market

❻ the"Typographer": slower than _____

❼ the first commercially sold typewriter: from a _____ inventor

❽ the first commercially sold typewriter: a _____ success in Europe

❶ machine

❷ impressions

❸ refrigerators

❹ 1575

❺ impractical

❻ handwriting

❼ Denmark

❽ commercial

石墨：皇室的象徵

> ▶▶ **影子跟讀「短段落」練習** 🎧 MP3 039

　　此篇為**「影子跟讀短段落練習」**，規劃了由聽**「短段落」**的 shadowing 練習，強化聽力專注力和掌握各個考點！

　　In 1812, a Massachusetts cabinet maker, William Monroe, made the first wooden pencil. The American pencil industry also took off during the 19th century. Starting with the Joseph Dixon Crucible Company, many pencil factories are based on the East Coast, such as New York or New Jersey. At first, pencils were all natural, unpainted and without printing company's names. Not until 1890s, many pencil companies started to paint pencils in yellow and put their brand name on it. Why yellow? Red or blue would look nice, too." You might think. It was actually a special way to tell the consumer that the graphite came from China.

　　1812 年，麻省的一個櫥櫃製造商，威廉‧莫瑞，製作了第一個木製鉛筆。美國製筆業也是在 19 世紀起飛。由約瑟夫‧狄克遜公司開始，很多鉛筆工廠都開在東岸，如紐約或新澤西州。起初，鉛筆都是天然的，沒有油漆，沒有印刷公司的名稱。直到 1890 年代，許多鉛筆公司開始把鉛筆漆成黃色，並把自己的品牌名稱印上。你可能會

認為「為什麼是黃色？紅色或藍色的也很好看。」。它實際上是用一種特殊的方式在告訴大家，石墨是來自中國。

It is because back in the 1800s, the best graphite in the world came from China. And the color yellow in China means royalty and respect. Only the imperial family was allowed to use the color yellow. Therefore, the American pencil companies began to paint their pencils bright yellow to show the regal feeling. Here we will be introducing Nicolas Jacques Conte who was credited as the inventor of the modern lead pencil from France.

這是因為早在 1800 年時，世界上最好的石墨來自中國。而在中國，黃色意味著皇室和尊重。只有皇室允許使用的黃色。因此，美國的鉛筆公司開始將自己的鉛筆漆成明亮的黃色，以顯示帝王的感覺。在這裡，我們將介紹尼古拉斯·雅克·康特，一位來自法國的現代鉛筆發明人。

此部分為**聽、讀雙效「填空」練習**，現在就一起動身，開始聽「短段落」，提升常考字彙、語感等答題能力！

In 1812, a Massachusetts 1._____, William Monroe, made the first 2._____. The American pencil industry also took off during the 19th century. Starting with the Joseph Dixon Crucible Company, many 3._____ are based on the East Coast, such as New York or 4._____.

At first, pencils were all natural, 5._____ and without printing company's names. Not until 1890s, many pencil companies started to paint pencils in 6._____ and put their brand name on it. Why yellow? 7._____ would look nice, too." You might think. It was actually a special way to tell the 8._____ that the 9._____ came from 10._____.

It is because back in the 1800s, the best graphite in the world came from China. And the color yellow in China means 11._____. Only the imperial family was allowed to use the color yellow. Therefore, the American pencil companies began to paint their pencils bright yellow to show the 12._____. Here we will be introducing Nicolas Jacques Conte who was credited as the 13._____ of the modern lead pencil from 14._____.

▶▶ 參考答案

1. cabinet maker
2. wooden pencil
3. pencil factories
4. New Jersey
5. unpainted
6. yellow
7. Red or blue
8. consumer
9. graphite
10. China
11. royalty and respect
12. regal feeling
13. inventor
14. France

❶ William Monroe: made the first wooden _____

❷ pencil factories: are based on the East Coast, such as _____
   _____ or New Jersey

❸ At first, pencils were all natural, _____ and without
   printing company's names.

❹ Not until 1890s: many pencil companies started to paint
   pencils in _____

❺ color: tell the consumer that the _____ came from
   China.

❻ The color yellow in China means _____ and respect.

❼ Only the _____ family was allowed to use the color
   yellow.

❽ the American pencil companies began to paint their pencils
   bright yellow to show the _____ feeling.

❶ pencil

❷ New York

❸ unpainted

❹ yellow

❺ graphite

❻ royalty

❼ imperial

❽ regal

UNIT 40

原子筆的潛力

　　此篇為「**影子跟讀短段落練習**」，規劃了由聽「**短段落**」的 shadowing 練習，強化聽力專注力和掌握各個考點！

　　The Birome was brought to the United States in 1945 by a mechanical pencil maker, Eversharp Co. Eversharp Co. and Eberhard Faner Co. teamed up and licensed the rights to sell the Birome ballpoint pen in the US.

　　Birome 原子筆在 1945 年由自動鉛筆公司 Eversharp 公司聯合 Eberhard Faner 公司拿下特許權，並在美國販售 Birome 原子筆。

　　At the same time, an American entrepreneur Milton Reynolds saw the potential of the ballpoint pen, and therefore founded the Reynolds International Pen Company. Both companies were doing great and ballpoint pen sales went rocket high in 1946, though people were still not 100% satisfied.

　　在同時，美國企業 家米爾頓-雷諾茲看到原子筆的潛力，並因

此成立了雷諾國際製筆公司。兩家公司都在做得非常好。原子筆銷量在 1946 年到達高峰，雖然人們仍然不是 100％滿意。

Another famous ballpoint pen maker was Marcel Bich. Bich was the founder of the famous pen company Bic we all recognize today. The Bic ballpoint pen has the history since 1953. Unlike most inventors, whose inventions were appreciated by the society when they were alive, John Jacob Loud did not.

另一個著名的圓珠筆製造商是馬塞爾–畢克。畢克是著名的筆公司 Bic 的創辦人。Bic 原子筆擁有自 1953 年以來的歷史。與大多數發明家不同的是，約翰勞德於生前的發明並未受到社會重視。

此部分為**聽、讀雙效「填空」練習**，現在就一起動身，開始聽「短段落」，提升常考字彙、語感等答題能力！

The Birome was brought to the 1.＿＿＿＿＿＿＿ in 1945 by a mechanical pencil 2.＿＿＿＿＿＿＿, Eversharp Co. Eversharp Co. and Eberhard Faner Co. teamed up and 3.＿＿＿＿＿＿＿ the rights to sell the Birome 4.＿＿＿＿＿＿＿ in the US. At the same time, an American 5.＿＿＿＿＿＿＿ Milton Reynolds saw the 6.＿＿＿＿＿＿＿ of the ballpoint pen, and therefore founded the Reynolds 7.＿＿＿＿＿＿＿ Pen Company. Both companies were doing great and ballpoint pen sales went 8.＿＿＿＿＿＿＿ high in 1946, though people were still not 9.＿＿＿＿＿＿＿ satisfied. Another 10.＿＿＿＿＿＿＿ ballpoint pen maker was Marcel Bich. Bich was the founder of the famous pen company. Bic we all recognize today. The Bic ballpoint pen has the 11.＿＿＿＿＿＿＿ since 1953. Unlike most inventors, whose inventions were appreciated by 12.＿＿＿＿＿＿＿ when they were alive, John Jacob Loud did not.

▶▶ 參考答案

1. United States	2. maker
3. licensed	4. ballpoint pen
5. entrepreneur	6. potential
7. International	8. rocket
9. 100%	10. famous
11. history	12. the society

❶ in 1945: The Birome was brought to the United States in 1945 by a _____ pencil maker

❷ Two companies teamed up and _____ the rights to sell the Birome ballpoint pen in the US.

❸ An American entrepreneur Milton Reynolds saw the _____ of the ballpoint pen

❹ in 1946: both companies were doing great and ballpoint pen sales went _____ high

❺ Another _____ ballpoint pen maker would be Marcel Bich

❻ Bich was the _____ of the famous pen company

❼ The Bic ballpoint pen has the _____ since 1953.

❽ John Jacob's inventions were _____ by the society

❶ mechanical

❷ licensed

❸ potential

❹ rocket

❺ famous

❻ founder

❼ history

❽ unappreciated

解雇促成了立可白發明

▶▶ **影子跟讀「短段落」練習** 🎧 MP3 041

此篇為**「影子跟讀短段落練習」**，規劃了由聽**「短段落」**的 shadowing 練習，強化聽力專注力和掌握各個考點！

Back in the late 90's while computers were not as common, liquid paper could be found in every pen case and on every desk. It is actually a brand name of the Newell Rubbermaid company that sells correction products. It is not a surprise that liquid paper was invented by a typist. Bette Graham who used to make many mistakes while working as a typist, invented the first correction fluid in her kitchen back in 1951. Using only paints and kitchen ware, Graham made her first generation correction fluid called Mistake Out and started to sell it to her co-workers.

在九零年代後期，當電腦還不普及時，你幾乎可以在每一個鉛筆盒，每一張桌子上看到立可白。它實際上是 Newell Rubbermaid 公司所銷售之修正產品的品牌名稱。立可白是由一位打字員所發明的，這並不意外。貝蒂・格雷厄姆在當打字員時經常發生錯誤。因此，在 1951 年時格雷厄姆在她的廚房裡，只利用了油漆及廚具，發明了她的第一代修正液，並且將它賣給自己的同事。

Graham for sure saw the business opportunity with her invention and founded the Mistake Out Company back in 1956 while she was still working as a typist. However, she was later on fired from her job because of some silly mistakes. Just like that, she worked from her kitchen alone for 17 years. In 1961, the company name was changed to Liquid Paper and it was sold to the Gillette Corporation for $47.5 million in 1979.

格雷厄姆肯定看到了這個發明的商機，在 1956 年她還在擔任打字員時便創辦了 Mistake Out 公司。爾後，她因為一些愚蠢的原因被公司解雇。就這樣，她在廚房裡獨自工作了 17 年。在 1961 年，該公司的名稱改為立可白，並在 1979 年以$47.5 百萬美元出售給吉列特公司。

此部分為**聽、讀雙效「填空」練習**，現在就一起動身，開始聽「短段落」，提升常考字彙、語感等答題能力！

　　Back in the late 90's 1._____ were not as common, 2._____ could be found in every pen case and on every 3._____. It is actually a 4._____ of the Newell Rubbermaid company that sells 5._____. It is not a surprise that liquid paper was invented by a 6._____. Bette Graham who used to make many 7._____ while working as a typist, invented the first correction 8._____ in her 9._____ back in 1951. Using only paints and 10._____, Graham made her first generation correction fluid called Mistake Out and started to sell it to her co-workers.

　　Graham for sure saw the 11._____ with her invention and founded the Mistake Out Company back in 1956 while she was still working as a typist. However, she was later on fired from her job because of some 12._____. Just like that, she worked from her kitchen alone for 13._____. In 1961, the company name was changed to Liquid Paper and it was sold to the Gillette Corporation for 14._____ in 1979.

▶▶ 參考答案

1. while computers

2. liquid paper

3. desk

4. brand name

5. correction products

6. typist

7. mistakes

8. fluid

9. kitchen

10. kitchen ware

11. business opportunity

12. silly mistakes

13. 17 years

14. $47.5 million

❶ in the late 90's: _____ could be found in every pen case

❷ the Newell Rubbermaid company: sells _____ products

❸ liquid paper: was invented by a _____

❹ Bette Graham: invented the first correction fluid in her _____ _____

❺ Mistake Out: sold to her _____

❻ Graham for sure saw the business _____ with her invention

❼ Graham was later on fired from her job because of some silly _____

❽ Liquid Paper: sold to the Gillette Corporation for _____ ___ million

❶ liquid paper

❷ correction

❸ typist

❹ kitchen

❺ co-workers

❻ opportunity

❼ mistakes

❽ 47.5

紙技術傳至歐洲

▶ 影子跟讀「短段落」練習 🎧 MP3 042

此篇為「**影子跟讀短段落練習**」，規劃了由聽「**短段落**」的 shadowing 練習，強化聽力專注力和掌握各個考點！

For a long time, the Chinese kept the paper manufacture as a secret to ensure a monopoly. However, after losing in a battle at the Talas River, the Chinese prisoners revealed the paper making technique to the Arabs which helped them build the first paper industry in Baghdad in 793 A.D. Interestingly, the Arabs also kept the first technique as a secret from the Europeans. As a result, the paper making technique did not reach Europe until hundreds of years later. Spain built the first European factory in 1150 A.D. Finally, after another 500 years, the first paper industry was built in Philadelphia in the USA. That is 1500 years after the first piece of paper was made!

長期以來，中國一直將造紙技術保密，以確保壟斷。然而公元 793 年，由於在失去塔拉斯河的戰役，中國戰俘透露製作技術並幫助阿拉伯人在巴格達建立了第一個造紙行業。有意思的是，阿拉伯人也將此技術保密。因此，造紙技術在幾百年後才傳到歐洲。西班牙在公

元 1150 年時建立了第一個歐洲的造紙廠，再過 500 年後美國的費城才建立了美國的第一個造紙廠。這是從第一張紙被發明算起的 1500 年後！

Around 2000 years ago, Cai Lun was born in Guiyang during the Han Dynasty. Because of his father's accusation, Cai was brought to the palace and got castrated at the age of 12. Even so, Cai loved to study and was designated to study along with the Emperor's son. He was a very hard-working person, so he was given several promotions under the rule of Emperor He. He was given the right to be in charge of manufacturing instruments and weapons.

大約 2000 多年前，蔡倫出生於漢朝的貴陽。由於他的父親犯罪，因此蔡被帶到了皇宮，在 12 歲時便被閹割。即便如此，蔡倫喜愛學習，所以被指定當作皇帝兒子的陪讀。他是一個很努力工作的人，因此在漢和帝的執政下被多次的升官。他被任命負責儀器及武器的製作。

此部分為**聽、讀**雙效「**填空**」練習，現在就一起動身，開始聽「短段落」，提升常考字彙、語感等答題能力！

For a long time, 1._____ kept the paper 2._____ as a secret to ensure 3._____. However, after losing in 4._____ at the Talas River, the Chinese 5._____ revealed the paper making 6._____ to the Arabs which helped them built the first paper 7._____ in Baghdad in 793 A.D. Interestingly, 8._____ also kept the first technique as a secret from 9._____. As a result, the paper making technique did not reach Europe until hundreds of years later. 10._____ built the first European factory in 1150 A.D. Finally, after another 500 years, the first 11._____ was built in 12._____ in the USA. That is 1500 years after the first piece of paper was made! Around 2000 years ago, Cai Lun was born in Guiyang during the 13._____. Because of his father's 14._____, Cai was brought to the 15._____ and got castrated at the age of 16._____. Even so, Cai loved to study and was designated to study along with the 17._____. He was a very hard working person , so he was given several 18._____ under the rule of Emperor He. He was given the right to be in charge of manufacturing instruments and weapons.

▶▶ 參考答案

1. the Chinese	2. manufacture
3. a monopoly	4. a battle
5. prisoners	6. technique
7. industry	8. the Arabs
9. the Europeans	10. Spain
11. paper industry	12. Philadelphia
13. Han Dynasty	14. accusation
15. palace	16. 12
17. Emperor's son	18. promotions

❶ paper manufacture: was kept as a secret to ensure a _____ _____.

❷ the Arabs knew the paper making technique from the _____ _____.

❸ in 793 A.D.: the Arabs built the first paper industry in _____ _____.

❹ in 1150 A.D.: _____ built the first European factory

❺ 500 years later: the first paper industry was built in _____ _____ in the USA.

❻ at the age of 12: Cai was brought to the palace and got _____ _____

❼ learning: Cai loved to study and was designated to study along with the Emperor's _____.

❽ under the rule of Emperor He: he got several _____

❶ monopoly

❷ prisoners

❸ Baghdad

❹ Spain

❺ Philadelphia

❻ castrated

❼ son

❽ promotions

底片的進展

此篇為「**影子跟讀短段落練習**」，規劃了由聽「**短段落**」的 shadowing 練習，強化聽力專注力和掌握各個考點！

Before digital photography became popular in the 21st century, photographic film was the dominant form of photography for hundreds of years. Without the invention of photographic film, movies would not be invented and many historical records would be much less realistic. The first flexible photographic roll of film was sold by George Eastman in 1885. It was a paper-based film. In 1889, the first transparent plastic roll film was invented. It was made of cellulose nitrate which is chemically similar to guncotton. It was quite dangerous because it was highly flammable.

在 21 世紀數位攝影開始流行前，底片是攝影數百年來的主要形式。如果沒有底片的發明，電影將不會被發明，眾多的歷史記錄也會較不真實。第一個柔性膠卷是由喬治・伊士曼於 1885 年售出。它是一種紙基膜。在 1889 年，第一個透明的塑料筒膜被發明出來。它是利用硝酸纖維素所製造，化學性質是類似於硝化纖維素。這其實是相

當危險的，因為它是高度易燃的。

Therefore, special storage was required. The first flexible movie films measured 35-mm wide and came in long rolls on a spool. Similar roll film for the camera was also invented in the mid 1920s. By the late 1920s, medium format roll film was created and had a paper backing which made it easy to handle in daylight.

因此，特殊的儲存方式是必要的。第一個柔性電影底片是 35 毫米寬，排列在長卷的捲筒上。相機類似的膠卷也在 1920 年代中期被發明出來。到了 1920 年代末期，中寬幅的底片被發明出來，它也有紙襯，使得它容易攜帶於日光下。

此部分為**聽、讀雙效「填空」練習**，現在就一起動身，開始聽「短段落」，提升常考字彙、語感等答題能力！

Before digital 1._____ became popular in the 21st century, 2._____ was the dominant form of photography for hundreds of years. Without the invention of photographic film, 3._____ would not be invented and many 4._____ would be much less realistic. The first flexible photographic 5._____ of film was sold by George Eastman in 1885. It was a 6._____ film. In 1889, the first 7._____ plastic roll film was invented. It was made of 8._____ nitrate which is chemically similar to 9._____. It was quite dangerous because it was highly flammable.

Therefore, special 10._____ was required. The first flexible movie films measured 11._____ and came in long rolls on a spool. Similar roll film for the 12._____ was also invented in the mid 1920s. By the late 1920s, medium 13._____ roll film was created and had 14._____ backing which made it easy to handle in daylight.

▶▶ 參考答案

1. photography

2. photographic film

3. movies

4. historical records

5. roll

6. paper-based

7. transparent

8. cellulose

9. guncotton

10. storage

11. 35-mm wide

12. camera

13. format

14. a paper

❶ Photographic _____ was the dominant form of photography for hundreds of years.

❷ Without the invention: there will be no _____

❸ Without the invention: historical records will be much less __ _____

❹ in 1885: The first _____ photographic roll of film was sold by George Eastman

❺ transparent plastic roll film: It was made of _____ nitrate

❻ chemical materials were dangerous so _____ was required.

❼ The first flexible movie films: _____ mm wide

❽ By the late 1920s: had a paper backing which made it easy to handle in _____ .

❶ film

❷ movies

❸ realistic

❹ flexible

❺ cellulose

❻ special storage

❼ 35

❽ daylight

燈泡的發展

　　此篇為「**影子跟讀短段落練習**」，規劃了由聽「**短段落**」的 shadowing 練習，強化聽力專注力和掌握各個考點！

　　If you think that Thomas Edison invented the first light bulb, you are technically wrong. There were several people who invented the light bulb, but Thomas Edison mostly got credited for it because he was the person who created the first practical light bulb that is available for the general public. 76 years before Thomas Edison filed the patten application for "Improvement in Electric Lights", Humphrey Davy invented an electric battery. When he connected wires to the battery and a piece of carbon, the carbon glowed. That was the first electric light ever invented.

　　如果你認為愛迪生發明第一個燈泡，嚴格上來說你是錯誤的。世上有幾個人發明了電燈泡，但湯瑪斯・愛迪生得到大部分的榮耀，因為他創造了第一個可用於一般大眾的實用電燈泡。早在湯瑪斯・愛迪生提出「電燈的改善」專利的 76 年之前，漢弗萊・戴維發明了電池。當他連接了導線、電池與一塊碳，碳發光了。這是首個電燈的發明。

Though it was not ready for the general use because the light didn't last long enough, and it was too bright for practical use. Years after, several other inventors tried to create light bulbs but no practical products were created. It was even made with platinum which the cost of platinum made it impractical for commercial use.

不過，由於無法長時間維持光亮，且光線太亮，所以這個發明還沒準備好被實際應用。幾年後，其他幾個發明家也試圖創造燈泡，但沒有實用的產品被創作出來。有人甚至提出用鉑作為材料，但鉑金的成本無法作為商業用途。

此部分為**聽、讀雙效「填空」練習**，現在就一起動身，開始聽「短段落」，提升常考字彙、語感等答題能力！

If you think that 1.＿＿＿＿＿＿＿ invented the first 2.＿＿＿＿＿＿＿, you are technically wrong. There were several people who invented the light bulb, but Thomas Edison mostly got credited for it because he was the person who created the first 3.＿＿＿＿＿＿＿ that is available for the 4.＿＿＿＿＿＿＿. 76 years before Thomas Edison filed the patten 5.＿＿＿＿＿＿＿ for "Improvement in Electric Lights", Humphrey Davy invented an 6.＿＿＿＿＿＿＿. When he connected wires to the 7.＿＿＿＿＿＿＿ and a piece of carbon, the carbon glowed. That was the first 8.＿＿＿＿＿＿＿ ever invented.

Though it was not ready for the general use because the light didn't last long enough, and it was too 9.＿＿＿＿＿＿＿ for practical use. Years after, several other 10.＿＿＿＿＿＿＿ tried to create light bulbs but no practical products were created. It was even made with platinum which the 11.＿＿＿＿＿＿＿ of platinum made it impractical for 12.＿＿＿＿＿＿＿.

▶▶ 參考答案

1. Thomas Edison	2. light bulb
3. practical light bulb	4. general public
5. application	6. electric battery
7. battery	8. electric light
9. bright	10. inventors
11. cost	12. commercial use

Part 1 生活類主題

Part 2 學術類主題

❶ Thomas Edison: got the _____ for inventing light bulb

❷ Thomas Edison: created the first _____ light bulb

❸ 76 years ago: Humphrey Davy invented an electric _____
____.

❹ For the carbon to glow, a connection should be made among _____, battery, and carbon

❺ the first electric light: too _____ for the general use

❻ the first electric light: too _____ for practical use

❼ Years after: _____ tried to create light bulbs

❽ platinum: not practical for commercial use due to the _____
_____

❶ credit

❷ practical

❸ battery

❹ wires

❺ short

❻ bright

❼ inventors

❽ cost

尿布

▶ 影子跟讀「短段落」練習 🎧 MP3 045

此篇為「**影子跟讀短段落練習**」，規劃了由聽「**短段落**」的 shadowing 練習，強化聽力專注力和掌握各個考點！

The diaper, one of the very first items that distinguished human from animals, was found being used from the Egyptians to the Romans. Though back then, people were using animal skins, leaf wraps, and other natural resources instead of the disposable diapers as we know today. The cotton "diaper like" progenitor was worn by the European and the American infants by the late 1800's. The shape of the progenitor was similar to the modern diaper but was held in place with safety pins. Back then, people were not aware of bacteria and viruses. Therefore, diapers were reused after drying in the sun. It was not until the beginning of the 20th century that people started to use boiled water in order to reduce common rash problems.

尿布是最早區分人類與動物的項目之一。從埃及人到羅馬人都有被發現使用尿布。雖然當時人們用獸皮、樹葉和其他自然資源包裹，與我們現今所知的紙尿布有所不同。尿布的前身在 1800 年底被歐洲

及美國的嬰兒所穿著。尿布前身的形狀設計非常類似現今的尿布，但卻是使用安全別針。那時，人們還沒有細菌和病毒的意識。因此，尿布曬乾後便再被重複使用。直到 20 世紀初，人們開始使用開水（燙尿布），這才減少了常見的皮疹問題。

However, due to World War II, cotton became a strategic material, so the disposable absorbent pad used as a diaper was created in Sweden in 1942. In 1946, Marion Donovan, a typical housewife from the United States invented a waterproof covering for diapers, called the "Boater." The model of the disposable diaper was made from a shower curtain. Back then, disposable diapers were only used for special occasions such as vacations because it was considered a "luxury item."

但由於第二次世界大戰，棉花成為了戰略物資，因此，拋棄式的尿布墊於 1942 年在瑞典被製作出來。1946 年，瑪麗安・唐納文，一位來自美國的典型家庭主婦發明了一種防水的尿布，她稱之為「船工」。她利用浴簾製作了紙尿布的模型。當時，紙尿布由於是被認為是奢侈品。

此部分為**聽、讀雙效「填空」練習**，現在就一起動身，開始聽「短段落」，提升常考字彙、語感等答題能力！

The 1._____, one of the very first 2._____ that distinguished human from 3._____, was found being used from the 4._____ to the 5._____. Though back then, people were using 6._____, leaf wraps, and other 7._____ instead of the 8._____ diapers as we know today. The cotton "diaper like" progenitor was worn by the European and the 9._____ by the late 1800's. The shape of the progenitor was similar to the modern diaper but was held in place with safety pins. Back then, people were not aware of 10._____. Therefore, diapers were reused after drying in the sun. It was not until the beginning of the 20th century that people started to use 11._____ in order to reduce common 12._____ problems.

However, due to World War II, cotton became a strategic material, so the disposable 13._____ pad used as a diaper was created in 14._____ in 1942. In 1946, Marion Donovan, a typical 15._____ from the United States invented a 16._____ covering for diapers, called the "Boater." The model of the disposable diaper was made from a 17._____. Back then, disposable diapers were only used for special occasions such as 18._____ because it was considered a "luxury item."

▶▶ 參考答案

1. diaper	2. items
3. animals	4. Egyptians
5. Romans	6. animal skins
7. natural resources	8. disposable
9. American infants	10. bacteria and viruses
11. boiled water	12. rash
13. absorbent	14. Sweden
15. housewife	16. waterproof
17. shower curtain	18. vacations

❶ The diaper: its use can be found in both _____ and the Romans

❷ back then: natural resources, including _____ and leaf wraps

❸ shape of the progenitor: held in place with _____ pins

❹ back then: people didn't have the awareness about _____ _____ and _____

❺ reused diaper: should be kept dry under the _____

❻ the 20th century: use _____ in order to reduce common rash problems

❼ World War II: _____ became a strategic material

❽ the Boater: had a _____ covering

❶ Egyptians

❷ animal skins

❸ safety

❹ bacteria, viruses

❺ sun

❻ boiled water

❼ cotton

❽ waterproof

動物玩耍

　　此篇為「影子跟讀短段落練習」，規劃了由聽「短段落」的 shadowing 練習，強化聽力專注力和掌握各個考點！

　　In today's lecture, we are going to cover more details concerning the play of young animals. The first type is locomotor play. As the word locomotor implies, this type of play strengthens muscle and physical coordination. The second type is predatory play, in which animals stalk and swoop upon playmates to mimic hunting behaviors. Even birds, such as falcons, crows, and swallows, engage in predatory play; they drop tiny objects from above and descend rapidly to catch those objects. The third type is object play, which is often played solitarily and combined with predatory play, though not always. For instance, primates, due to their adroitness, play with various objects in a similar way as human children do. Primates have been proven to demonstrate their imagination in object play. In research, a chimpanzee having been trained to use sign language placed a purse on his foot, and gave the sign for "shoe". The fourth type of play is social play, which allows animals to form friendship, learn cooperation, and mimic adult competitive behaviors without acting violently. Regarding the benefits of play, I would like to focus on the effects on the brain. Emotionally, play just makes animals feel relaxed and less stressed. They touch one another the most when playing, and touching stimulates a chemical in the brain called opiate, which generates a soothing feeling. To sum up, there are at least four areas that play exerts positive effects on: physical, social, emotional, and intelligent areas.

今天的講課，我們將涵蓋更多關於年輕動物玩耍的細節。第一種類型是運動玩耍。就像運動這個字暗示的，這個類型加強肌肉和身體協調能力。第二種類型是捕食玩耍，玩耍當中動物會尾隨並突然襲擊玩伴，這是在模仿打獵行為。甚至鳥類，例如獵鷹、烏鴉和燕子，也會進行捕食玩耍。他們會從高處丟下小型物體，然後快速下降去抓那些物體。第三個類型是物體玩耍，常常是獨自進行並和捕食玩耍合併，雖然不見得總是這樣。例如，由於靈長類的肢體靈巧，他們玩各種物體的方式和人類小孩玩耍的方式是類似的。在進行物體玩耍時，靈長類已經被證實會展現想像力。在一個研究中，一隻曾受過手語訓練的黑猩猩將一個皮包放在腳上，並比出「鞋子」的手語。第四個類型是社交玩耍，讓動物建立友誼，學習合作，並模仿成年競爭性的行為，但不會展現暴力。關於玩耍的益處，我想專注在對頭腦的影響。情緒上，玩耍就是讓動物覺得放鬆，比較沒壓力。當玩耍時，他們碰觸彼此最多，而碰觸會刺激腦內一種稱為鴉片類物質的化學物質，這化學物質會產生放鬆的感覺。總之，玩耍至少在四個方面發揮正面效應：生理、社交、情緒和智能方面。

此部分為**聽、讀雙效「填空」練習**，現在就一起動身，開始聽「短段落」，提升常考字彙、語感等答題能力！

In today's lecture, we are going to cover more details concerning the play of young 1._____. The first type is locomotor play. As the word locomotor implies, this type of play strengthens 2._____ and physical 3._____. The second type is 4._____ play, in which animals stalk and swoop upon 5._____ to mimic hunting 6._____. Even birds, such as 7._____, crows, and swallows, engage in predatory play; they drop tiny 8._____ from above and 9._____ rapidly to catch those objects. The third type is object play, which is often played 10._____ and combined with predatory play, though not always. For instance, 11._____, due to their 12._____, play with various objects in a similar way as human children do. Primates have been proven to demonstrate their 13._____ in object play. In research, a 14._____ having been trained to use sign 15._____ placed a purse on his foot, and gave the sign for "shoe". The fourth type of play is social play, which allows animals to form 16._____, learn 17._____, and mimic adult 18._____ behaviors without acting 19._____. Regarding the benefits of play, I would like to focus on the 20._____ on the brain. Emotionally, play just makes animals feel relaxed and less 21.__

_____. They touch one another the most when playing, and touching stimulates a 22._____ in the brain called opiate, which 23._____ a soothing feeling. To sum up, there are at least four areas that play exerts positive effects on: physical, social, emotional, and 24._____ areas.

▶▶ 參考答案

1. animals	2. muscle
3. coordination	4. predatory
5. playmates	6. behaviors
7. falcons	8. objects
9. descend	10. solitarily
11. primates	12. adroitness
13. imagination	14. chimpanzee
15. language	16. friendship
17. cooperation	18. competitive
19. violently	20. effects
21. stressed	22. chemical
23. generates	24. intelligent

❶ locomotor: strengthens muscle and physical _____

❷ predatory play: swoop upon playmates to mimic hunting _____ _____

❸ birds: _____, crows, and swallows, engage in predatory play

❹ object play: primates possess _____

❺ In research: a _____ having been trained to use sign language

❻ social play: develop traits, such as friendship, cooperation, and _____

❼ brain: touching stimulates a _____

❽ four areas: physical, social, emotional, and _____ areas.

❶ coordination

❷ behaviors

❸ falcons

❹ adroitness

❺ chimpanzee

❻ imitation

❼ chemical

❽ intelligent

伍迪・艾倫的電影

▶▶ 影子跟讀「短段落」練習 🎧 MP3 047

此篇為「**影子跟讀短段落練習**」，規劃了由聽「**短段落**」的 shadowing 練習，強化聽力專注力和掌握各個考點！

Renowned American director and comedian, Woody Allen, became an octogenarian in 2015, meaning he is in his 80s. The younger generation of audiences might not be so familiar with his early career, although many have acquainted themselves with Woody Allen's more recent movies set in major European cities, such as *Match Point*, set in London and released in 2005, *Midnight in Paris*, released in 2011, and *To Rome with Love*, released in 2012. It is true that the highly-acclaimed director made a major comeback to the cinema with those movies, particularly with *Midnight in Paris*, which not only won him the Academy Award for Best Original Screenplay and the Golden Globe Award for Best Screenplay, but also attained the highest box office revenue in North America among all of Woody Allen's movies. It is fair to say that Woody Allen is a natural born comedian. His involvement in comedy started very early at the age of 15 when he began writing jokes for comedians performing on Broadway, and at age 20 in

1955, he was hired by The NBC Comedy Hour in Los Angeles as a full-time writer for many comedy shows. Since then, he has remained a prolific writer, having written numerous TV show scripts, short stories, works of comic fiction, and screenplays. He extended his caliber to stand-up comedy in the 1960s, performing as a stand-up comedian in nightclubs in Manhattan. Allen became well-known nationwide in 1965, when he had his own TV show, "The Woody Allen Show".

　　知名的美國導演及喜劇演員，伍迪・艾倫，在 2015 年已經八十歲了。較年輕的觀眾可能對他早期的職涯不是很熟悉，雖然很多人熟悉伍迪・艾倫近年來將場景設在歐洲主要城市的電影，例如場景在倫敦並於 2005 年上映的《愛情決勝點》、2011 年上映的《午夜巴黎》及 2012 年上映的《愛上羅馬》。的確，這位備受讚賞的導演以這些電影成功地重返大螢幕，尤其是他不但因《午夜巴黎》得到奧斯卡金像獎最佳原創劇本獎及金球獎最佳劇本獎，而且《午夜巴黎》在北美洲的票房獲利是伍迪・艾倫所有的電影裡最高的。若說伍迪・艾倫是天生的喜劇演員應該不為過。他和喜劇的關係早在 15 歲就開始了，他那時開始替在百老匯表演的喜劇演員寫笑話，在 1955 年他 20 歲時，洛杉磯 NBC 電視台的喜劇節目雇用他為全職作家，他為許多喜劇秀寫劇本。自此之後，他一直是位多產的作家，寫下眾多電視節目腳本，短篇故事，喜劇小説和電影劇本。在 1960 年代，他的才華延伸到單人脫口秀，他在曼哈頓的夜間俱樂部表演。在 1965 年，艾倫有了他個人的電視節目：伍迪・艾倫秀，此時他成為全國知名的人物。

此部分為**聽、讀雙效「填空」練習**，現在就一起動身，開始聽「短段落」，提升常考字彙、語感等答題能力！

Renowned American 1.＿＿＿＿＿＿ and 2.＿＿＿＿＿＿＿, Woody Allen, became an 3.＿＿＿＿＿＿ in 2015, meaning he is in his 80s. The younger generation of 4.＿＿＿＿＿＿ might not be so familiar with his early 5.＿＿＿＿＿＿, although many have acquainted themselves with Woody Allen's more recent movies set in major 6.＿＿＿＿＿＿ cities, such as *Match Point*, set in 7.＿＿＿＿＿＿ and released in 2005, *Midnight in Paris*, released in 2011, and *To Rome with Love*, released in 2012. It is true that the highly-acclaimed director made a major 8.＿＿＿＿＿＿ to the cinema with those movies, particularly with *Midnight in Paris*, which not only won him the Academy Award for Best Original Screenplay and the Golden Globe Award for Best Screenplay,...... It is fair to say that Woody Allen is a 9.＿＿＿＿＿＿ born comedian. His 10.＿＿＿＿＿＿ in comedy started very early at the age of 15 when he began writing jokes for comedians performing on Broadway, and at age 11.＿＿＿＿＿＿ in 1955, he was hired by The NBC Comedy Hour in Los Angeles as a full-time 12.＿＿＿＿＿＿ for many comedy shows. Since then, he has remained a 13.＿＿＿＿＿＿ writer, having written 14.＿＿＿＿＿＿ TV show scripts, short stories, works of comic 15.＿＿＿＿＿＿, and screenplays. He extended his 16.＿＿＿＿＿＿ to stand-up comedy in the 1960s, performing as a stand-up comedian in nightclubs in 17._____. Allen became well-known 18._____ in 1965, when he had his own TV show, "The Woody Allen Show".

▶▶ 參考答案

1. director	2. comedian
3. octogenarian	4. audiences
5. career	6. European
7. London	8. comeback
9. natural	10. involvement
11. 20	12. writer
13. prolific	14. numerous
15. fiction	16. caliber
17. Manhattan	18. nationwide

❶ Woody Allen: became an _____ in 2015

❷ *Midnight in Paris*, released in _____

❸ *To Rome with Love*, released in _____

❹ at the age of 15: His involvement in _____

❺ at age 20: was hired as a full-time _____

❻ Since then, he has remained a _____ writer

❼ He performed as a stand-up comedian in _____ in Manhattan

❽ in 1965: Allen became well-known _____

❶ octogenarian

❷ 2011

❸ 2012

❹ comedy

❺ writer

❻ prolific

❼ nightclubs

❽ nationwide

知名華裔美籍建築師貝聿銘

▶ 影子跟讀「短段落」練習 🎧 MP3 048

    As Pei's secondary education in Shanghai drew near an end, he decided to enter an American university, a decision which he once admitted was made under the influence of Bing Crosby movies, in which college life in America seemed full of fun. Though he soon found out that the rigorous academic life differed drastically from the portrayal in movies, he excelled in the architecture school of the Massachusetts Institute of Technology (MIT). Particularly, he was drawn to the school of modern architecture, featuring simplicity and the utilization of glass and steel materials, and influenced by architect Frank Lloyd Wright. In 1961, he began designing the Mesa Laboratory for the National Center for Atmospheric Research in Colorado. The Mesa Laboratory embodied his philosophy akin to Organic Architecture. The building rests harmoniously in the Rocky Mountains, as if sculpted out of rocks. Then, after President John F. Kennedy's assassination in 1963, Pei was chosen by Ms. Kennedy to design the John F. Kennedy Presidential Library and Museum, which includes a large square glass-enclosed courtyard with a triangular tower and a circular walkway. Following some remarkable architectures in the U.S., such as Dallas City Hall, the Hancock Tower in Boston and the National Gallery East Building in Washington, D.C., Pei executed the most challenging project in his career in the 1980s, the renovation of the Louvre Museum in Paris. His decision to build a huge glass and steel pyramid at the center of the courtyard initially ignited controversy, yet since its completion, the glass pyramid has become a famous landmark in Paris and Pei's most representative work.

貝聿銘從在上海就讀的高中快畢業時，他決定到美國念大學。他曾承認這個決定是受到賓‧克洛斯比的電影影響，在那些電影裡，美國的大學生活似乎是充滿了歡樂。雖然他很快就發現嚴格的學術生活和電影的描繪相差甚多，他就讀於麻省理工學院的建築系時表現得非常優秀。他尤其被現代建築吸引，現代建築的特色是極簡風和運用玻璃及鋼鐵素材，他也被法蘭克‧洛伊‧萊特影響。在 1961，他開始替位於科羅拉多州的國家大氣研究中心設計麥莎實驗室大樓。麥莎實驗室大樓展現了類似有機建築的哲學。這棟建築物和諧地和洛磯山脈並存，看起來像是直接從岩石雕鑿出來的。之後，在 1963 年甘迺迪總統被刺殺後，甘迺迪夫人選擇貝聿銘為甘迺迪總統圖書館及紀念館做設計。此圖書館及紀念館包含一大片被玻璃環繞的方形中庭、三角錐狀的高塔和圓形的走道。在美國完成一些知名建築之後，例如達拉斯市政廳、波士頓的漢考克大廈和首府華盛頓的國家美術館東側大樓，貝聿銘於 1980 年代執行了職業生涯中最具挑戰性的案子，就是巴黎羅浮宮博物館的翻新工程。他決定在羅浮宮中庭的中央建造一座巨型玻璃和鋼鐵金字塔，這個決定最初引起爭議，但是玻璃金字塔完成後，它成為巴黎知名的地標，也是貝聿銘最具代表性的作品。

此部分為**聽、讀雙效「填空」練習**，現在就一起動身，開始聽「短段落」，提升常考字彙、語感等答題能力！

As Pei's secondary 1.＿＿＿＿＿＿＿ in Shanghai drew near an end, he decided to enter an American 2.＿＿＿＿＿＿＿, a decision which he once admitted was made under the 3.＿＿＿＿＿＿ of Bing Crosby movies, in which college life in America seemed full of fun. Though he soon found out that the 4.＿＿＿＿＿＿ academic life differed 5.＿＿＿＿＿＿＿ from the 6.＿＿＿＿＿＿＿ in movies, he excelled in the 7.＿＿＿＿＿＿＿ school of the Massachusetts Institute of Technology (MIT). Particularly, he was drawn to the school of 8.＿＿＿＿＿＿＿ architecture, featuring 9.＿＿＿＿＿＿＿ and the utilization of 10.＿＿＿＿＿＿ and 11.＿＿＿＿＿＿＿ materials, and influenced by architect Frank Lloyd Wright. Throughout his 12.＿＿＿＿＿＿＿, Pei has designed numerous 13.＿＿＿＿＿＿＿ buildings. In 1961, he began designing the Mesa 14.＿＿＿＿＿＿＿ for the National Center for 15.＿＿＿＿＿＿＿ Research in Colorado. The Mesa Laboratory embodied his 16.＿＿＿＿＿＿＿ akin to Organic Architecture. The building rests 17.＿＿＿＿＿＿＿ in the Rocky Mountains, as if sculpted out of rocks. Then, after President John F. Kennedy's 18.＿＿＿＿＿＿＿ in 1963, Pei was chosen by Ms. Kennedy to design the John F. Kennedy Presidential Library and Museum, which includes a large square glass-enclosed 19.＿＿＿＿＿＿＿ with a triangular tower and a circular walkway. ......, the

20._____ of the Louvre Museum in Paris. His decision to build a huge glass and steel 21._____ at the center of the courtyard initially ignited 22._____, yet since its completion, the glass pyramid has become a famous landmark in Paris and Pei's most representative work.

▶▶ 參考答案

1. education
2. university
3. influence
4. rigorous
5. drastically
6. portrayal
7. architecture
8. modern
9. simplicity
10. glass
11. steel
12. career
13. notable
14. Laboratory
15. Atmospheric
16. philosophy
17. harmoniously
18. assassination
19. courtyard
20. renovation
21. pyramid
22. controversy

❶ Pei : enter an American _____ after his secondary education

❷ a stark contrast between rigorous academic life and the ____ _____ in movies

❸ modern architecture: simplicity and the utilization of _____ _____ and _____ materials

❹ designing the Mesa Laboratory: rests _____ in the Rocky Mountains

❺ in 1963: President John F. Kennedy's _____

❻ Kennedy Presidential Library and Museum: a large _____ ____ with a triangular tower

❼ the most challenging project: the _____ of the Louvre Museum

❽ decision: a huge glass and steel _____ at the center

❶ university

❷ portrayal

❸ glass, steel

❹ harmoniously

❺ assassination

❻ courtyard

❼ renovation

❽ pyramid

塗鴉藝術

▶▶ **影子跟讀「短段落」練習** 🎧 MP3 049

　　此篇為**「影子跟讀短段落練習」**，規劃了由聽**「短段落」**的 shadowing 練習，強化聽力專注力和掌握各個考點！

　　Graffiti has existed for as long as written words have existed, with examples traced back to Ancient Greece, Ancient Egypt, and the Roman Empire. In fact, the word graffiti came from the Roman Empire. Some even consider cave drawings by cavemen in the Neolithic Age the earliest form of graffiti, and thus make it the longest existent art form. Basically, graffiti refers to writing or drawings that have been scrawled, painted, or sprayed on surfaces in public in an illicit manner. The general functions of graffiti include expressing personal emotions, recording historical events, and conveying political messages. Nevertheless, today graffiti has found its place in mainstream art, and for many graffiti artists, their works have become highly commercialized and lucrative. Contemporary artistic graffiti has just arisen in the past twenty five years in the inner city of New York, with street artists painting and writing illegitimately on public buildings, street signs or public transportation, more commonly on the exteriors of subway trains. These artists experimented with different styles and mediums, such as sprays and stencils. The difference between artistic graffiti and traditional graffiti is that the former has evolved from scribbling on a wall to a complex and skillful form of personal and political expression. Graffiti artists have also branched out to collaborate with fashion designers and produce numerous products, increasing the daily and global presence of this art form. In the U. S., many graffiti artists have extended their careers to skateboard, apparel, and shoe design for companies such as DC Shoes, Adidas, and Osiris.

　　塗鴉的歷史就跟文字的歷史一樣久，塗鴉的例子可追溯到古希臘、古埃及和羅馬帝國。事實上，graffiti 這個字發源自羅馬帝國。有些人甚至將新石器時代的穴居人所畫的洞穴壁畫視為塗鴉最早的形式，使得塗鴉成為現存最久的藝術。基本上，塗鴉指的是未經法律許可在公共領域的壁面上潦草書寫，畫畫或噴漆形成的文字或圖案。塗鴉的主要功能包括表達個人情緒，記錄歷史事件，及傳達政治訊息。然而，今日塗鴉已經在主流藝術中取得一席之地，而且對許多塗鴉藝術家而言，他們的作品已經被高度商業化並帶來高度利潤。當今的藝術性塗鴉是在過去二十五年間於紐約市中心興起的，當時街頭藝術家未經法律許可就在公共建築、馬路上的標誌或公共運輸工具上面畫畫及寫字，比較普遍的是畫在地鐵車廂的外層。這些藝術家實驗不同的風格和媒介，例如噴漆和金屬模板。藝術性塗鴉和傳統塗鴉的差異在於前者已從在牆壁上潦草畫畫進化成表達個人和政治意涵的複雜及高技術的型式。塗鴉藝術家也和流行服飾設計師合作拓展出許多產品，提高此藝術在日常生活和全球的能見度。在美國，許多塗鴉藝術家已經將職涯延伸到滑板、服裝及鞋子設計，他們替 DC Shoes、愛迪達和 Osiris 等品牌設計。

此部分為**聽、讀雙效「填空」練習**，現在就一起動身，開始聽「短段落」，提升常考字彙、語感等答題能力！

Graffiti has existed for as long as written words have existed, with examples traced back to Ancient 1._____, Ancient 2._____, and the Roman Empire. In fact, the word graffiti came from the Roman Empire. Some even consider cave drawings by 3._____ in the Neolithic Age the earliest form of graffiti, and thus make it the longest 4._____ art form. Basically, graffiti refers to writing or drawings that have been scrawled, painted, or sprayed on 5._____ in public in an 6._____ manner. The 7._____ functions of graffiti include expressing 8._____ emotions, recording 9._____ events, and conveying 10._____ messages. Nevertheless, today graffiti has found its place in 11._____ art, and for many graffiti artists, their works have become highly 12._____ and lucrative. Contemporary artistic graffiti has just arisen in the past twenty five years in the inner city of New York, with street artists painting and writing 13._____ on public buildings, street signs or public 14._____, more commonly on the exteriors of 15._____ trains. These artists experimented with different styles and 16._____, such as sprays and stencils. The difference between artistic graffiti and traditional graffiti is that the former has evolved from 17._____ on a wall to a complex and 18._____ form of personal and political expression....... In the U. S., many graffiti artists have extended their careers to 19._____, 20._____, and shoe design for companies such as DC Shoes, Adidas, and Osiris.

▶▶ 參考答案

1. Greece	2. Egypt
3. cavemen	4. existent
5. surfaces	6. illicit
7. general	8. personal
9. historical	10. political
11. mainstream	12. commercialized
13. illegitimately	14. transportation
15. subway	16. mediums
17. scribbling	18. skillful
19. skateboard	20. apparel

❶ Graffiti: can be traced back to three countries, including Greece, _____, and the Roman Empire

❷ prehistoric time: cave drawings by _____

❸ graffiti: writing or drawings in an _____ manner

❹ functions: expressing personal _____

❺ street artists: painting and writing illegitimately on the exteriors of _____ trains

❻ experimentation: with different styles and mediums, such as sprays and _____

❼ collaboration: with _____ designers

❽ graffiti artists: have extended their careers to _____, _____ , and shoe design

❶ Egypt

❷ cavemen

❸ illicit

❹ emotions

❺ subway

❻ stencils

❼ fashion

❽ skateboard, apparel

反烏托邦的文學

▶▶ 影子跟讀「短段落」練習 🎧 MP3 050

　　此篇為**「影子跟讀短段落練習」**，規劃了由聽**「短段落」**的 shadowing 練習，強化聽力專注力和掌握各個考點！

　　In today's popular culture, the idea of dystopia is gaining more popularity in young adult fiction and Hollywood movies, as the success of the novels and movies of *The Hunger Games* series has demonstrated. In fact, we can trace the origin of dystopian literature way back to 1605, to a satire in Latin called *Mundus Alter et Idem*, meaning "an old world and a new", written by Joseph Hall, Bishop of Norwich, England. *An Old World and a New* satirizes life in London and customs of the Roman Catholic Church. It also served as an inspiration to Jonathan Swift's *Gulliver's Travels*. Speaking of Jonathan Swift's *Gulliver's Travels*, some of you might consider it utopian fiction. Well, it is both utopian and dystopian. *Gulliver's Travels* illustrates utopian and dystopian places. Or a dystopia might be disguised as a utopia, forming an ambiguous genre. One example is Samuel Butler's *Erewhon*, which consists of utopian and dystopian traits. In the 20th century, the most famous dystopian works of fiction are probably Aldous Huxley's *Brave New World*, written in 1931 and George Orwell's *1984*, written in 1949. It is not hard to understand that the characteristics of dystopia contribute to its popularity in popular fiction and movies. Those characteristics tend to create tension and anxiety, factors that draw contemporary audience. Those include totalitarian control of citizens, a bureaucratic government, restriction of freedom and information, as well as constant surveillance on civilians with technology. Civilians' individuality and equality are abolished, while a central figurehead or bureaucracy exerts dictatorial control over society. Other traits are associated with doomsday, such as poverty, hunger, and the destruction of nature.

　　在今日的流行文化中，反烏托邦的概念在青少年小說和好萊塢電影中越來越受歡迎，如同《飢餓遊戲》的小說和電影之成功已經證明了。事實上，我們能追溯反烏托邦文學的起源至 1605 年，是一本名為 *Mundus Alter et Idem* 的拉丁文諷刺小說，書名的意思是「一個舊世界和新世界」，作者是約瑟夫・霍爾，他是英國諾威治的主教。《一個舊世界和新世界》嘲諷倫敦的生活型態及羅馬天主教的習俗。這本書也啟發了強納森・斯威夫特的《格列佛遊記》。提到強納森・斯威夫特的《格列佛遊記》，你們有些人可能把它視為烏托邦小說。嗯，它是烏托邦，也是反烏托邦小說。烏托邦和反烏托邦地區《格列佛遊記》都描述了。或者反烏托邦可能表面上假裝成烏托邦，形成一種模糊的文學類型。一例是在山謬・巴特勒的《烏有之鄉》裡，兩個種類的特色都並存。二十世紀最有名的反烏托邦小說應該是艾爾道斯・赫胥黎 1931 年的著作《美麗新世界》和喬治・歐威爾 1949 年的著作《1984》。不難理解，反烏托邦的特色導致了這個概念在流行小說和電影中非常普遍。那些特色會創造緊繃和焦慮感，這些都是吸引當代

觀眾的因素。特色包括對公民的獨裁控制，官僚化政府，對自由和資訊的限制，及不斷用科技監視人民。人民的個人特色和平等權被剝奪了，而一位中央領導或官僚體系以獨裁方式控制社會。其他特色跟末日有關聯，例如貧窮、飢餓和對大自然的破壞。

▶▶ 聽、讀雙效「填空」練習 🎧 MP3 050

此部分為**聽、讀雙效「填空」練習**，現在就一起動身，開始聽「短段落」，提升常考字彙、語感等答題能力！

In today's popular culture, the idea of dystopia is gaining more popularity in young adult 1.＿＿＿＿＿＿＿ and Hollywood movies, as the success of the novels and movies of *The Hunger Games* series has demonstrated. In fact, we can trace the origin of dystopian 2.＿＿＿＿＿＿＿ way back to 1605, to a 3.＿＿＿＿＿＿＿＿ in Latin called *Mundus Alter et Idem*, meaning "an old world and a new", written by Joseph Hall, Bishop of Norwich, England. ......it is both utopian and dystopian. *Gulliver's Travels* illustrates utopian and dystopian places. Or a dystopia might be disguised as a utopia, forming an 4.＿＿＿＿＿＿＿ genre. One example is Samuel Butler's *Erewhon*, which consists of utopian and dystopian 5.＿＿＿＿＿＿＿. In the 20th century, the most famous dystopian works of fiction are 6.＿＿＿＿＿＿＿ Aldous Huxley's *Brave New World*, written in 1931 and George Orwell's *1984*, written in 1949. It is not hard to understand that the 7.＿＿＿＿＿＿＿ of dystopia 8._____ to its popularity in popular fiction and movies. Those characteristics tend to create 9._____ and 10._____, factors that draw 11._____ audience. Those include 12._____ control of citizens, a 13._____ government, 14._____ of freedom and 15._____, as well as constant 16._____ on civilians with technology. Civilians' individuality and 17._____ are 18._____, while a central figurehead or 19._____ exerts dictatorial control over society. Other traits are associated with doomsday, such as 20._____, hunger, and the destruction of nature.

▶▶ 參考答案

1. fiction	2. literature
3. satire	4. ambiguous
5. traits	6. probably
7. characteristics	8. contribute
9. tension	10. anxiety
11. contemporary	12. totalitarian
13. bureaucratic	14. restriction
15. information	16. surveillance
17. equality	18. abolished
19. bureaucracy	20. poverty

❶ the idea: gaining more popularity in young adult _____ __ and Hollywood movies

❷ origin of dystopian: can be traced back to a _____

❸ *An Old World and a New*: an _____ to Jonathan Swift's *Gulliver's Travels*

❹ Swift's fiction: both _____ and dystopian

❺ Aldous Huxley's *Brave New World*, written in _____

❻ characteristics of dystopia: create tension and _____

❼ traits: constant _____ on civilians with technology

❽ two things are abolished: _____ and equality

❶ fiction

❷ satire

❸ inspiration

❹ utopian

❺ 1931

❻ anxiety

❼ surveillance

❽ individuality

國家圖書館出版品預行編目(CIP)資料

雅思聽力聖經 / Amanda Chou著. -- 初版. --
新北市：倍斯特出版事業有限公司, 2021.
04　面；　公分. -- (考用英語系列；031)
ISBN 978-986-06095-1-6(平裝附光碟片)
1.國際英語語文測驗系統 2.考試指南

805.189　　　　　　　　　　110004019

考用英語系列　031

雅思聽力聖經（附英式發音MP3）

初　　版　　2021年4月
定　　價　　新台幣460元

作　　者　　Amanda Chou
出　　版　　倍斯特出版事業有限公司
發 行 人　　周瑞德
電　　話　　886-2-8245-6905
傳　　真　　886-2-2245-6398
地　　址　　23558 新北市中和區立業路83巷7號4樓
E - m a i l　　best.books.service@gmail.com
官　　網　　www.bestbookstw.com
總 編 輯　　齊心瑀
特約編輯　　陳韋佑
封面構成　　高鍾琪
內頁構成　　菩薩蠻數位文化有限公司
印　　製　　大亞彩色印刷製版股份有限公司

港澳地區總經銷　　泛華發行代理有限公司
地　　址　　香港新界將軍澳工業邨駿昌街7號2樓
電　　話　　852-2798-2323
傳　　真　　852-3181-3973